D0064906

DRIVING BLIND

Books by Ray Bradbury

DRIVING BLIND

Ray Bradbury

AVON BOOKS  NEW YORK

DRIVING BLIND is an original publication of Avon Books. This work has never before appeared in book form. This is a collection of fiction. Any similarity to actual persons or events is entirely coincidental.

Page 261 is an extension of this copyright page.

AVON BOOKS
A division of
The Hearst Corporation
1350 Avenue of the Americas
New York, New York 10019

Collection copyright © 1997 by Ray Bradbury
Interior design by Kellan Peck
Visit our website at **http://AvonBooks.com**
ISBN: 0-380-97381-2

Library of Congress Cataloging in Publication Data:

Bradbury, Ray, 1920–
    Driving blind / Ray Bradbury.—1st ed.
        p.   cm.
    1. United States—Social life and customs—20th century—Fiction.
I. Title.
PS3503.R167D75   1997   97-4378
813'.54—dc21   CIP

First Avon Books Printing: October 1997

AVON TRADEMARK REG. U.S. PAT. OFF. AND IN OTHER COUNTRIES, MARCA REGISTRADA, HECHO EN U.S.A.

Printed in the U.S.A.

FIRST EDITION

QPM   10   9   8   7   6   5   4   3   2   1

With undying love to
the early-arriving granddaughters,
JULIA, CLAIRE, GEORGIA
and MALLORY.

And to
the late-arriving grandsons,
DANIEL, CASEY-RAY, SAMUEL
and THEODORE.

Live forever!

Contents

CONTENTS

DRIVING BLIND

Night Train to Babylon

J ames Cruesoe was in the club car of a train plummeting out of Chicago, rocking and swaying as if it were drunk, when the conductor, lurching by, glanced at the bar, gave Cruesoe a wink, and lurched on. Cruesoe listened.

Uproars, shouts and cries.

That is the sound, he thought, of sheep in panic, glad to be fleeced, or hang gliders, flung off cliffs with no wings.

He blinked.

For there at the bar, drawn to a blind source of joyous consternation, stood a cluster of men glad for highway robbery, pleased to have wallets and wits purloined.

That is to say: gamblers.

Amateur gamblers, Cruesoe thought, and rose to stagger down the aisle to peer over the shoulders of businessmen behaving like high school juniors in full stampede.

"Hey, watch! The Queen *comes!* She *goes. Presto! Where?"*

"There!" came the cry.

"Gosh," cried the dealer. "Lost my shirt! Again! Queen up, Queen gone! Where?"

He'll let them win twice, Cruesoe thought. Then spring the trap.

"There!" cried all.

"Good gravy!" shouted the unseen gambler. "I'm sunk!"

Cruesoe had to look, he *yearned* to see this agile vaudeville magician.

On tiptoe, he parted a few squirming shoulders, not knowing what to expect.

But there sat a man with no fuzzy caterpillar brows or waxed mustaches. No black hair sprouted from his ears or nostrils. His skull did not poke through his skin. He wore an ordinary dove-gray suit with a dark gray tie tied with a proper knot. His fingernails were clean but unmanicured. Stunning! An ordinary citizen, with the serene look of a chap about to lose at cribbage.

Ah, yes, Cruesoe thought, as the gambler shuffled his cards slowly. That carefulness revealed the imp under the angel's mask. A calliope salesman's ghost lay like a pale epidermis below the man's vest.

"Careful, gents!" He fluttered the cards. "Don't bet too much!"

Challenged, the men shoveled cash into the furnace.

"Whoa! No bets above four bits! Judiciously, sirs!"

The cards leapfrogged as he gazed about, oblivious of his deal.

"Where's my left thumb, my right? Or are there *three thumbs?*"

They laughed. What a jokester!

"Confused, chums? Baffled? Must I lose *again?*"

"Yes!" all babbled.

"Damn," he said, crippling his hands. "'Damn! Where's the Red Queen? Start over!'"

"No! The *middle* one! *Flip* it!"

The card was flipped.

"Ohmigod," someone gasped.

"Can't look." The gambler's eyes were shut. "How much did I lose *this* time?"

"Nothing," someone whispered.

"Nothing?" The gambler, aghast, popped open his eyes.

They all stared at a black card.

"Gosh," said the gambler. "I thought you *had* me!"

His fingers spidered to the right, another black card, then to the far left. The Queen!

"Hell," he exhaled, "why's she *there?* Christ, guys, keep your cash!"

"No! No!" A shaking of heads. "You won. You couldn't help it. It was just—"

"Okay. If you insist! Watch out!"

Cruesoe shut his eyes. This, he thought, is the end. From here on they'll lose and bet and lose again. Their fever's up.

"Sorry, gents. Nice try. *There!*"

Cruesoe felt his hands become fists. He was twelve again, a fake mustache glued to his lip and his school chums at a party and the three-card monte laid out. "Watch the Red Queen *vanish!*" And the kids shout and laugh as his hands blurred to win their candy but hand it back to show his love.

"One, two, *three! Where can she *be?*"

He felt his mouth whisper the old words, but the voice was the voice of this wizard stealing wallets, counting cash on a late-night train.

"Lost again? God, fellas, quit before your wife shoots you! Okay, Ace of spades, King of clubs, Red Queen. You won't see *her* again!"

"No! *There!*"

Cruesoe turned, muttering. *Don't listen! Sit!* Drink! Forget your twelfth birthday, your friends. Quick!

He took one step when:

"That's *three* times lost, pals. I *must* fold my tent and . . ."

"No, no, don't leave *now!* We got to win the damn stuff back. Deal!"

And as if struck, Cruesoe spun about and returned to the madness.

"The Queen was *always* there on the left," he said.

Heads turned.

"'It was there all the *time*," Cruesoe said, louder.

"And who are you, sir?" The gambler raked in the cards, not glancing up.

"A boy magician."

"Christ, a boy magician!" The gambler riffled the deck.

The men backed off.

Cruesoe exhaled. "I know how to do the three-card monte."

"Congratulations."

"I won't cut in, I just wanted these good men—"

There was a muted rumble from the good men.

"—to know *anyone* can win at the three-card monte."

Looking away, the gambler gave the cards a toss.

"Okay, wisenheimer, deal! Gents, your bets. Our friend here takes over. Watch his hands."

Cruesoe trembled with cold. The cards lay waiting.

"Okay, son. Grab on!"

"I can't *do* the trick well, I just know *how* it's *done*."

"Ha!" The gambler stared around. "Hear that, chums? Knows how it *works*, but can't *do*. *Right?*"

Cruesoe swallowed. "Right. But—"

"But? Does a cripple show an athlete? A dragfoot pace the sprinter? Gents, you want to change horses out here—" He glanced at the window. Lights flashed by. "—halfway to Cincinnati?"

The gents glared and muttered.

"Deal! Show us how you can steal from the poor."

Cruesoe's hands jerked back from the cards as if burnt.

"You prefer not to cheat these idiots in my presence?" the gambler asked.

5

Clever beast! Hearing themselves so named, the idiots roared assent.

"Can't you see what he's *doing?*" Cruesoe said.

"Yeah, yeah, we see," they babbled. "Even-steven. Lose some, win some. Why don't you go back where you came from?"

Cruesoe glanced out at a darkness rushing into the past, towns vanishing in night.

"Do you, sir," said the Straight-Arrow gambler, "in front of all these men, accuse me of raping their daughters, molesting their wives?"

"No," Cruesoe said, above the uproar. "Just cheating," he whispered, "at cards!"

Bombardments, concussions, eruptions of outrage as the gambler leaned forward.

"Show us, sir, where these cards are inked, marked, or stamped!"

"There *are* no marks, inks, or stamps," Cruesoe said. "It's all prestidigitation."

Jesus! He might as well have cried *Prostitution!*

A dozen eyeballs rolled in their sockets.

Cruesoe fussed with the cards.

"Not marked," he said. "But your hands aren't connected to your wrists or elbows and finally all of it's not connected to . . ."

"To *what*, sir?"

"Your heart," Cruesoe said, dismally.

The gambler smirked. "This, sir, is not a romantic excursion to Niagara Falls."

"Yah!" came the shout.

A great wall of faces confronted him.

"I," Cruesoe said, "am very tired."

He felt himself turn and stagger off, drunk with the sway of the train, left, right, left, right. The conductor saw him coming and punched a drift of confetti out of an already punched ticket.

"Sir," Cruesoe said.

The conductor examined the night fleeing by the window.

"Sir," Cruesoe said. "Look *there*."

The conductor reluctantly fastened his gaze on the mob at the bar, shouting as the cardsharp raised their hopes but to dash them again.

"Sounds like a good time," the conductor said.

"*No*, sir! Those men are being cheated, fleeced, buggywhipped—"

"Wait," said the conductor. "Are they disturbing the peace? Looks more like a birthday party."

Cruesoe shot his gaze down the corridor.

A herd of buffalo humped there, angry at the Fates, eager to be shorn.

"Well?" said the conductor.

"I want that man thrown off the train! Don't you see what he's up to? That trick's in every dime-store magic book!"

The conductor leaned in to smell Cruesoe's breath.

"Do you *know* that gambler, sir? Any of his pals your friends?"

"No, I—" Cruesoe gasped and stopped. "My God, I just realized." He stared at the conductor's bland face.

"*You*," he said, but could not go on.

You are in cohoots, he thought. You share the moola at the end of the line!

"Hold *on*," said the conductor.

He took out a little black book, licked his fingers, turned pages. "Uh-huh," he said. "Lookit all the biblical/Egyptian names. *Memphis*, Tennessee. *Cairo*, Illinois? Yep! And here's one just ahead. Babylon."

"Where you throw that cheat *off*?"

"No. Someone *else*."

"You wouldn't do that," Cruesoe said.

"No?" said the conductor.

Cruesoe turned and lurched away. "Damn idiot stupid fool," he muttered. "Keep your smart-ass mouth *shut!*"

"Ready, gentlemen," the insidious cardsharp was shouting. "Annie over. *Flea*-hop! Oh, *no!* The bad-news boy is *back!*"

Jeez, hell, damn, was the general response.

"Who do you think you *are*?" Cruesoe blurted.

"Glad you asked." The gambler settled back, leaving the cards to be stared at by the wolf pack. "Can you guess where I'm going tomorrow?"

"South America," Cruesoe said, "to back a tin-pot dictator."

"Not bad." The sharpster nodded. "Go on."

"Or you are on your way to a small European state where some nut keeps a witch doctor to suck the economy into a Swiss bank."

"The boy's a poet! I have a letter here, from Castro."

His gambler's hand touched his heart. "And one from Bothelesa, another from Mandela in South Africa. Which do I choose? Well." The gambler glanced at the rushing storm outside the window. "Choose any pocket, right, left, inside, out." He touched his coat.

"Right," Cruesoe said.

The man shoved his hand in his right coat pocket, pulled out a fresh pack of cards, gave it a toss.

"Open it. That's it. Now riffle and spread. *See* anything?"

"Well . . ."

"Gimme." He took it. "The next monte will be from the deck *you* choose."

Cruesoe shook his head. "That's not how the trick works. It's how you *lay down* and *pick up* the cards. *Any* deck would do."

"Pick!"

Cruesoe picked two tens and a red Queen.

"Okay!" The gambler humped the cards over each other. "Where's the Queen?"

"Middle."

He flipped it over. "Hey, you're good." He smiled.

"You're better. That's the trouble," Cruesoe said.

"Now, see this pile of ten-dollar bills? That's the stake, just put by these gents. You've stopped the game too long. Do you join or be the skeleton at the feast?"

"Skeleton."

"Okay. They're off! There she goes. Queen here, Queen there. Lost! *Where?* You ready to risk all your cash, fellows? Want to pull *out? All* of a single *mind?*"

9

Fierce whispers.

"*All*," someone said.

"No!" Cruesoe said.

A dozen curses lit the air.

"Smart-ass," said the cardsharp, his voice deadly calm, "do you realize that your static may cause these gentlemen to lose *everything?*"

"No," Cruesoe said. "It's not my static. *Your* hands deal the cards."

Such jeers. Such hoots. "Move! My God, move!"

"Well." With the three cards still under his clean fingers the gambler stared at the rushing storm beyond the window. "You've ruined it. Because of you, their choice is doomed. You and only you have intruded to burst the ambience, the aura, the bubble that enclosed this game. When I turn the card over my friends may hurl you off the train."

"They wouldn't do that," Cruesoe said.

The card was turned over.

With a roar the train pulled away in a downpour of rain and lightning and thunder. Just before the car door slammed, the gambler thrust a fistful of cards out on the sulfurous air and tossed. They took flight: an aviary of bleeding pigeons, to pelt Cruesoe's chest and face.

The club car rattle-banged by, a dozen volcanic faces with fiery eyes crushed close to the windows, fists hammering the glass.

His suitcase stopped tumbling.

The train was gone.

He waited a long while and then slowly bent and began to pick up fifty-two cards. One by one. One by one.

A Queen of hearts. Another Queen. Another Queen of hearts. And one more.

A Queen . . .

Queen.

Lightning struck. If it had hit him, he would never have known.

If MGM Is Killed,
Who Gets the Lion?

"**H**oly Jeez, damn. Christ off the cross!" said Jerry Would.

"Please," said his typist-secretary, pausing to erase a typo in a screenplay, "I have Christian ears."

"Yeah, but my tongue is Bronx, New York," said Would, staring out the window. "Will you just look, take one long fat look at *that!*"

The secretary glanced up and saw what he saw, beyond.

"They're repainting the studio. That's Stage One, isn't it?"

"You're damn right. Stage One, where we built the *Bounty* in '34 and shot the Tara interiors in '39 and Marie Antionette's palace in '34 and now, for God's sake, look what they're doing!"

"Looks like they're changing the number."

"Changing the number, hell, they're wiping it *out!*

13

No more One. Watch those guys with the plastic over-
lays in the alley, holding up the goddamn pieces, trying
them for size."

The typist rose and took off her glasses to see better.

"That looks like UGH. What does 'Ugh' mean?"

"Wait till they fit the first letter. See? Is that or is
that not an H?"

"H added to UGH. Say, I bet I know the rest.
Hughes! And down there on the ground, in small letters, the stencil? 'Aircraft'?"

"Hughes Aircraft, dammit!"

"Since when are we making planes? I know the
war's on, but—"

"We're not making any damn planes," Jerry Would
cried, turning from the window.

"We're shooting air combat films, then?"

"No, and we're not shooting no damn air films!"

"I don't see . . ."

"Put your damn glasses back on and look. Think!
Why would those SOBs be changing the number for a
name, hey? What's the big idea? We're not making an
aircraft carrier flick and we're not in the business of
tacking together P-38s and—Jesus, *now* look!"

A shadow hovered over the building and a shape
loomed in the noon California sky.

His secretary shielded her eyes. "I'll be damned,"
she said.

"You ain't the only one. You wanna tell me what
that thing is?"

She squinted again. "A balloon?" she said. "A barrage balloon?"

"You can say that again, but *don't!*"

She shut her mouth, eyed the gray monster in the sky, and sat back down. "How do you want this letter addressed?" she said.

Jerry Would turned on her with a killing aspect. "Who gives a damn about a stupid letter when the world is going to hell? Don't you get the full aspect, the great significance? Why, I ask you, would MGM have to be protected by a barrage—hell, there goes *another!* That makes *two* barrage balloons!"

"*No* reason," she said. "We're not a prime munitions or aircraft target." She typed a few letters and stopped abruptly with a laugh. "I'm slow, right? We *are* a prime bombing target?"

She rose again and came to the window as the stencils were hauled up and the painters started blowgunning paint on the side of Stage One.

"Yep," she said, softly, "there it is. AIRCRAFT COMPANY. HUGHES. When does he move *in?*"

"What, Howie the nut? Howard the fruitcake? Hughes the billionaire bastard?"

"*That* one, yeah."

"He's going nowhere, he still has his pants glued to an office just three miles away. Think! Add it up. MGM is here, right, two miles from the Pacific coast, two blocks away from where Laurel and Hardy ran their tin lizzie like an accordion between trolley cars in 1928!

And three miles north of us and *also* two miles in from the ocean is—"

He let her fill in the blanks.

"Hughes Aircraft?"

He shut his eyes and laid his brow against the window to let it cool. "Give the lady a five-cent seegar."

"I'll be damned," she breathed with revelatory delight.

"You ain't the only one."

"When the Japs fly over or the subs surface out beyond Culver City, the people painting that building and re-lettering the signs hope that the Japs will think Clark Gable and Spencer Tracy are running around Hughes Aircraft two miles north of here, making pictures. And that MGM, *here,* has Rosie the Riveters and P-38s flying out of that hangar down there all day!"

Jerry Would opened his eyes and examined the evidence below. "I got to admit, a sound stage does look like a hangar. A hangar looks like a sound stage. Put the right labels on them and invite the Japs *in. Banzai!*"

"Brilliant," his secretary exclaimed.

"You're fired," he said.

"What?"

"Take a letter," said Jerry Would, his back turned.

"Another letter?"

"To Mr. Sid Goldfarb."

"But he's right upstairs."

"Take a letter, dammit, to Goldfarb, Sidney. Dear Sid. Strike that. Just Sid. I am damned angry. What the hell is going on? I walk in the office at eight a.m. and it's MGM. I walk out to the commissary at noon and Howard Hughes is pinching the waitresses' behinds. Whose bright idea was this?"

"Just what *I* wondered," his secretary said.

"You're fired," said Jerry Would.

"Go on," she said.

"Dear Sid. Where was I? Oh, yeah. Sid, why weren't we informed that this camouflage would happen? Remember the old joke? We were all hired to watch for icebergs sailing up Culver Boulevard? Relatives of the studio, uncles, cousins? And now the damned iceberg's here. And it wears tennis shoes, a leather jacket, and a mustache over a dirty smile. I been here twelve years, Sidney, and I refuse—aw, hell, finish typing it. Sincerely. No, not sincerely. Angrily yours. Angrily. Where do I sign?"

He tore the letter from the machine and whipped out a pen.

"Now take this upstairs and throw it over the transom."

"Messengers get killed for messages like this."

"Killed is better than fired."

She sat quietly.

"Well?" he said.

"I'm waiting for you to cool down. You may want to tear this letter up, half an hour from now."

"I will not cool down and I will not tear up. Go."

And still she sat, watching his face until the lines faded and the color paled. Then very quietly she folded the letter and tore it across once and tore it across twice and then a third and fourth time. She let the confetti drift into the trash basket as he watched.

"How many times have I fired you today?" he said.

"Just three."

"Four times and you're out. Call Hughes Aircraft."

"I was wondering when you—"

"Don't wonder. Get."

She flipped through the phone book, underlined a number, and glanced up. "Who do you want to talk to?"

"Mr. Tennis Shoes, Mr. Flying Jacket, the billionaire butinsky."

"You really think he ever answers the phone?"

"Try."

She tried and talked while he gnawed his thumbnail and watched them finish putting up and spraying the AIRCRAFT stencil below.

"Hell and damn," she said at last, in total surprise. She held out the phone. "He's *there!* And answered the phone *himself!*"

"You're putting me on!" cried Jerry Would.

She shoved the phone out in the air and shrugged.

He grabbed it. "Hello, who's this? What? Well, say, Howard, I mean Mr. Hughes. Sure. This is MGM Studios. My name? Would. Jerry Would. You *what?* You heard me? You saw *Back to Broadway?* And *Glory Years.* But sure, you once owned RKO Studios, right? Sure, sure. Say, Mr. Hughes, I got a little problem here. I'll make this short and sweet."

He paused and winked at his secretary.

She winked back. The voice on the line spoke nice and soft.

"What?" said Jerry Would. "Something's going on over at *your* place, *too?* So you know why I'm calling, sir. Well, they just put up the aircraft letters and spelled out HUGHES on Stage One. You like that, huh? Looks great. Well, I was wondering, Howard, Mr. Hughes, if you could do me a little favor."

Name it, said the quiet voice a long way off.

"I was thinking if the Japs come with the next tide by air or by sea and no Paul Revere to say which, well, when they see those big letters right outside my window, they're sure going to bomb the hell outta what they think is P-38 country and Hughes territory. A brilliant concept, sir, brilliant. Is *what?* Is everyone here at MGM happy with the ruse? They're not dancing in the streets but they do congratulate you for coming up with such a world-shaking plan. Now here's my point. I gotta lot of work to finish. Six films shooting, two films editing, three films starting. What I need is a nice safe place to work, you got the idea? That's it. Yeah. That's it. You got a nice small corner of one of your hangars that—sure! You're way ahead of me. I should *what?* Yeah, I'll send my secretary over right after lunch with some files. You got a typewriter? I'll leave mine here. Boy, How—Mr. Hughes, you're a peach. Now, tit for tat, if *you* should want to move into *my* office here? Just joking. Okay. Thanks. Thanks. Okay. She'll be there, pronto."

And he hung up.

His secretary sat stolidly, examining him. He looked away, refused to meet her stare. A slow blush moved up his face.

"*You're* fired," she said.

"Take it easy," he said.

She rose, gathered a few papers, hunted for her purse, applied a perfect lipstick mouth, and stood at the door.

"Have Joey and Ralph bring all the stuff in that top file," she said. "That'll do for starters. You coming?"

"In a moment," he said, standing by the window, still not looking at her.

"What if the Japs figure out this comedy, and bomb the *real* Hughes Aircraft instead of this fake one?"

"Some days," sighed Jerry Would, "you can't win for losing."

"Shall I write a letter to Goldfarb to tell him where you're going?"

"Don't write, call. That way there's no evidence."

A shadow loomed. They both looked up at the sky over the studio.

"Hey," he said, softly, "there's another. A *third* balloon."

"How come," she said, "it looks like a producer I used to know?"

"You're—" he said.

But she was gone. The door shut.

Hello, I Must Be Going

There was a quiet tapping at the door and when Steve Ralphs opened it there stood Henry Grossbock, five foot one inches tall, immaculately dressed, very pale and very perturbed.

"Henry!" Steve Ralphs cried.

"Why do you sound like that?" Henry Grossbock said. "What have I done? Why am I dressed like this? Where am I going?"

"Come in, come in, someone might see you!"

"Why does it matter if someone *sees* me?"

"Come in, for God's sake, don't stand there arguing."

"All right, I'll come in, I have things to talk about anyway. Stand aside. There. I'm in."

Steve Ralphs backed off across the room and waved to a chair. "Sit."

"I don't feel welcome." Henry sat. "You have any strong liquor around this place?"

"I was just thinking that." Steve Ralphs jumped, ran into the kitchen, and a minute later returned with a tray, a bottle of whiskey, two glasses, and some ice. His hands were trembling as he poured the liquor.

"You look shaky," said Henry Grossbock. "What's wrong?"

"Don't you know, can't you *guess?* Here."

Henry took the glass. "You sure poured me a lot."

"You're going to need it. Drink."

They drank and Henry examined his coat front and his sleeves.

"You still haven't told me where I am going," he said, "or have I been there already? I don't usually dress this way except for concerts. When I stand up there before an audience, well, one desires respect. This is very good scotch. Thanks. Well?"

He stared at Steve Ralphs with a steady and penetrating stare.

Steve Ralphs gulped half of his drink and put it down and shut his eyes. "Henry, you've already been to a far place and just come back, for God's sake. And now you'll have to return to that place."

"What place, *what* place, stop the riddles!"

Steve Ralphs opened his eyes and said, "How did you get here? Did you take a bus, hire a taxi, or . . . walk from the graveyard?"

"Bus, taxi, walk? And what's that about a graveyard?"

"Henry, drink the rest of your drink. Henry, you've been in that graveyard for years."

"Don't be silly. What would I be doing *there?* I never applied for any—" Henry stopped and slowly sank back in his chair. "You mean—?"

Steve Ralphs nodded. "Yes, Henry."

"Dead? And in the graveyard? Dead and in the graveyard four years? Why didn't someone *tell* me?"

"It's hard to tell someone who's dead that he *is.*"

"I see, I see." Henry finished his drink and held the glass out for more. Steve Ralphs refilled.

"Dear, dear," said Henry Grossbock, slowly. "My, my. So *that's* why I haven't felt up to snuff lately."

"That's why, Henry. Let me catch up." Steve Ralphs poured more whiskey in his own glass and drank.

"So that's why you looked so peculiar when you opened the door just now—"

"That's why, Henry."

"Sorry. I really didn't mean—"

"Don't get up, Henry. You're here now."

"But under the circumstances—"

"It's all right. I'm under control. And even given the circumstances, you were always my best friend and it's nice, in a way, to see you again."

"Strange. *I* wasn't shocked to see *you.*"

"There's a difference, Henry. I mean, well—"

"You're alive, and I'm not, eh? Yes, I can see that. Hello, I must be going."

"What?"

"Groucho Marx sang a song with that title."

"Oh, yeah. Sure."

23

"Marvelous man. Funny. Is he still around? Did he die, too?"

"I'm afraid so."

"Don't be afraid. I'm not. Don't know why. Just now." Henry Grossbock sat up straight. "To business."

"What business?"

"Told you at the front door. Important. Must tell. I am very upset."

"So was I, but this liquor does wonders. Okay, Henry, shoot."

"The thing is—" Henry Grossbock said, finishing his second drink quickly, "my wife is neglecting me."

"But Henry, it's perfectly natural—"

"Let me finish. She used to come visit constantly. Brought me flowers, put a book nearby once, cried a lot. Every day. Then every other day. Now, never. How do you explain that? Refill, please."

Steve Ralphs tipped the bottle.

"Henry, four years is a long *time*—"

"You can say that again. How about Eternity, there's a *real* vaudeville show."

"You didn't really expect to be entertained, did you?"

"Why not? Evelyn always spoiled me. She changed dresses two or three times a day because she knew I loved it. Haunted bookshops, brought me the latest, read me the oldest, picked my ties, shined my shoes, her women's-lib friends joshed her for *that*. Spoiled. Yes, I expected to have someone fill the time for me."

"That's not how it works, Henry."

Henry Grossbock thought and nodded, solemnly, and sipped his whiskey. "Yes, I guess you're right. But let me name the *biggest* problem."

"What's that?"

"She's stopped crying. She used to cry every night, every day at breakfast, twice in the afternoon, just before supper. Then, lights out, crying."

"She missed you, Henry."

"And now she doesn't?"

"Time heals all wounds, they say."

"I don't want this wound healed. I liked things just the way they were. A good cry at dawn, a half decent cry before tea, a final one at midnight. But it's over. Now I don't feel wanted or needed."

"Think about it the way you had to think about your honeymoon with Evelyn. It had to end sometime."

"Not entirely. There were stray bits of it for the rest of forty years."

"Yes, but you *do* see the resemblance?"

"Honeymoon ended. Life over. I certainly don't much care for the residue." A thought struck Henry Grossbock. He set his glass down, sharply. "Is there someone *else?*"

"Someone . . ."

"*Else!* Has she taken up with—?"

"And what if she has?"

"How *dare* she!"

"Four years, Henry, four years. And no, she hasn't taken up with anyone. She'll remain a widow for the rest of her life."

"That's more like it. I'm glad I came to see you first. Set me straight. So she's still single and—hold on. How come no more tears at midnight, crying at breakfast?"

"You didn't really expect that, did you?"

"But damn, I miss it. A man's got to have *something!*"

"Don't you have any friends over at the—" Steve Ralphs stopped, flushed, refilled his glass, refilled Henry's.

"You were going to say graveyard. Bad lot, those. Layabouts. No conversation."

"You were always a great talker, Henry."

"Yes, yes, that's so, wasn't I? *Aren't* I? And you were my best listener."

"Talk some more, Henry. Get it all out."

"I think I've hit the high points, the important stuff. She's stopped coming by. That's bad. She's stopped crying. That's the very worst. The lubricant that makes—what I have become—worth the long while. I wonder if I showed up, would she cry again?"

"You're *not* going to visit?"

"Don't think I should, eh?"

"Nasty shock. Unforgivable."

"*Who* wouldn't forgive me?"

"Me, Henry. *I* wouldn't."

"Yes, yes. Oh dear. My, my. Good advice from my best friend."

"Best, Henry." Steve Ralphs leaned forward. "You *do* want her to get over you, don't you?"

"No! Yes. No! God, I don't know. Yes, I guess so."

"After all she *has* missed you and cried every day for most of four years."

"Yes." Henry Grossbock nursed his glass. "She *has* put in the time. I suppose I *should* let her off the hook."

"It would be a kindness, Henry."

"I don't *feel* kind, I don't *want* to be kind, but hell, I'll be kind anyhow. I do love the dear girl."

"After all, Henry, she has lots of years ahead."

"True. Damn. Think of it. Men age better but die younger. Women live longer but age badly. Strange arrangement God has made, don't you agree?"

"Why don't you ask Him, now that you're there?"

"Who, God? An upstart like me? Well, well. Ummm." Henry sipped. "Why not? What's she up to? If she's not dashing about in open cars with strange men, *what?*"

"Dancing, Henry. Taking dance lessons. Sculpting. Painting."

"Always wanted to do that, never could. Concert schedules, cocktail parties for possible sponsors, recitals, lectures, travel. She always said *someday.*"

"Someday is here, Henry."

"Took me by surprise, is all. Dancing, you say? Sculpting? Is she any good?"

"A fair dancer. A *very* fine sculptor."

"Bravo. Or is it brav*a*? Yes. Brava. I think I'm glad for that. Yes, I *am* glad. Fills the time. And what do *I* do? Crosswords."

"Crosswords?"

"Dammit, what else is there, considering my cir-

27

cumstances? Fortunately, I recall every single good and bad puzzle ever printed in the *New York Times* or the *Saturday Review.* Crossword. Short nickname, three letters, for Tutankhamen. Tut! Four letters, one of the Great Lakes. *Erie!* Easy, that one. Fourteen letters, old Mediterranean capital. Hell. Constantinople!"

"Five letters. Word for best pal, good friend, fine husband, brilliant violinist."

"Henry?"

"Henry. You." Steve Ralphs smiled, lifted his glass, drank.

"That's my cue to grab my hat and leave. Oh, I didn't bring a hat. Well, well."

Steve Ralphs suddenly swallowed very hard.

"What's this?" said Henry, leaning forward, listening.

"A repressed sob, Henry."

"Good! That's better. Warms the old heart, *that* does. I don't suppose you could—"

"Suppress a few more sobs, once or twice a week for the next year?"

"I hesitate to ask—"

"I'll try, Henry." Another mysterious sound moved up Steve Ralph's throat. He hastened to lid it with whiskey. "Tell you what. I'll call Evelyn, say I'm writing a book about you, need some of your personal books, notes, golf clubs, spectacles, the lot, bring them here, and, well, once a week, anyway, look them over, feel sad. How's *that* sound?"

"That's the ticket, or what are friends for?" Henry

Grossbock beamed. There was color in his cheeks. He drank and stood up.

At the door, Henry turned and peered into Steve Ralph's face.

"Dear me, dear me, are those tears?"

"I think so, Henry."

"Well now, that's more like it. Not Evelyn's of course, and you're not heaving great sobs. But it'll do. Much thanks."

"Don't mention it, Henry."

"Well." Henry opened the door. "See you around."

"Not too soon, Henry."

"Eh? No, of course not. No hurry. Good-bye, friend."

"Oh, good-bye, Henry." Yet another mysterious gulp arose in the younger man's throat.

"Yes, yes." Henry smiled. "Keep that up until I'm down the hall. Well, as Groucho Marx said—"

And he was gone. The door shut.

Turning, slowly, Steve Ralphs walked to the telephone, sat down, and dialed.

After a moment the receiver on the other end clicked and a voice spoke.

Steve Ralphs wiped his eyes with the back of his hand and at last said:

"Evelyn?"

House Divided

Small fifteen-year-old fingers plucked at the buttons on Chris' trousers like a moth drawn to a flame. He heard whispered words in the dark room that meant nothing, and could not be remembered a moment after they were spoken.

Vivian's lips were so fresh that it was unbelievable. Chris had the feeling that this was a dream. This was a pantomime carried out in the dark, which he could not see. Vivian herself had switched out every light. It had started as every evening like it had started. With Chris and his brother Leo climbing upstairs with Vivian and Shirley, their girl cousins. The girls were both blonde and smiling. Leo was sixteen and clumsy. Chris was twelve and knew nothing of such moths darting in the warm pantomime, or that there was a light shining in him he had never known about, that some girl might want. Shirley was ten, going on eleven, but very curious. Vivian was the ringleader; she was fifteen and beginning to see the world's people.

Chris and Leo had arrived in the family car, acting properly grave, since it was such a grave situation. They walked silently behind Mother and Dad into the Johnsons' house on Buttrick Street, where all the other relatives were gathered in a hushed spell of waiting. Uncle Inar sat by the phone, looking at it, his big hands twitching all by themselves, uneasy animals in his lap.

It was like walking into the hospital itself. Uncle Lester was very badly off. They were waiting for news now from the hospital. Lester had been shot in the stomach on a hunting trip and had lingered half-alive for three days now. So they had come tonight to be together, just in case they received the news of their Uncle Lester's passing. All three sisters and Lester's two brothers were there, with their wives and husbands and children.

After a proper interval of hushed speaking, Vivian had very carefully suggested, "Mama, we'll go upstairs and tell ghost stories, so you grown-ups can talk."

"Ghost stories," said Uncle Inar vaguely. "What a thing to tell tonight. Ghost stories."

Vivian's mama agreed. "You can go upstairs if you're quiet. We don't want any racket."

"Yes, ma'am," said Chris and Leo.

They left the room, walking slowly on the edge of their shoes. Nobody noticed their going. They could have been several phantoms passing for all the attention they got.

Upstairs, Vivian's room had a low couch against one wall, a dressing table with pink-folded silk for a skirt, and flower pictures. There was a green leather diary, fabulously inscribed but securely padlocked on the table, freckles of powder on it. The room smelled sweetly soft and nice.

They sat upon the couch, backs lined neatly against the wall, a row of solemn ramrods, and Vivian, like always, told the first ghost story. They turned out all but one lamp, which was very feeble, and she put her voice low in her rounded breasts and whispered it out.

It was that ancient tale about lying abed late one night, with stars cold in the sky, al alone in a big old house when some *thing* starts creeping slowly up the stairs to your room. Some strange and awful visitor from some other world. And as the story advanced, slowly step by step, step by step, your voice got more tense and more whispery and you kept waiting and waiting for that shocking finale.

"*It* crept up to the second step, it stepped up to the third step, it came to the fourth step . . ."

All four of their hearts had churned to this story a thousand times. Now, again, a cold sweat formed on four anticipatory brows. Chris listened, holding Vivian's hand.

"The strange sounds came on to the sixth step, and rustled to the seventh step, and then to the eighth step . . ."

Chris had memorized the story, often, and told it often, but no one could tell it quite like Vivian. She was

33

husking it now, like a witch, eyes half shut, body tensed against the wall.

Chris went over the story in his mind, ahead of her. "Ninth, tenth, and eleventh steps. Twelve, thirteen, fourteen steps. *It* came to the *top* of the stairs . . ."

Vivian went on. "Now it's in the hall at the top of the stairs. Outside the door. Now it's coming inside. Now it's closing the door." A pause. "Now it's walking across your room. Now it's passing the bureau. Now it's over your bed. Now it's standing right over you, right over your head . . ."

A long pause, during which the darkness of the room got darker. Everybody drew in their breath, waiting, waiting.

"*I GOTCHA!*"

Screaming, then giggling, you burst out! You let the black bat crash into the web. You had built the web of tension and horror so completely inside, minute by minute, step by step, around and around, like a very dainty horrible spider weaving, and in that tumultuous climax when I GOTCHA! flew out at you, like a sickening bat, it shattered the web down in trembling apprehension and laughter. You had to laugh to cover up your old old fear. You shrieked and giggled, all four of you. You hollered and shook the couch and held onto each other. Oh that familiar old story! You rocked back and forth, shivering, breathing fast. Funny how it still scared you after the hundredth telling.

The giggling subsided quickly. Footsteps, real ones, were hurrying up the steps to Vivian's room. By the sound of them Chris knew it was Auntie. The door opened.

"Vivian," cried Auntie. "I told you about noise! Don't you have any respect!"

"All right, Mama. We're sorry."

"I'm sorry, Auntie," said Chris, meaning it. "We just forgot ourselves. We got scared."

"Vivian, you keep them quiet," directed Auntie, her scowl softening. "And if I hear you again you'll all come downstairs."

"We'll be good," said Leo, quietly, earnestly.

"Well, all right, then."

"Has the hospital called?" asked Shirley.

"No," said Auntie, her face changing, remembering. "We expect to hear soon."

Auntie went downstairs. It took another five minutes to get back into the spell of storytelling.

"Who'll tell a story now?" asked Shirley.

"Tell another one, Vivian," said Leo. "Tell the one about the butter with the evil fungus in it."

"Oh, I tell that *every* time," said Vivian.

"I'll tell one," said Chris. "A *new* one."

"Swell," said Vivian. "But let's turn out the other light first. It's too light in here."

She bounced up, switched out the last light. She came back through the utter dark and you could smell her coming and feel her beside you, Chris realized. Her hand grabbed his, tightly. "Go on," she said.

"Well . . ." Chris wound his story up on a spool,

getting it ready in his mind. "Well, once upon a
time—"

"Oh, we heard *that* one before!" they all laughed.
The laughter came back from the unseen wall of the
room. Chris cleared his throat and started again.

"Well, once upon a time there was a black castle in
the woods—"

He had his audience immediately. A castle was a
darn nice thing to start with. It wasn't a bad story he
had in mind, and he would have told it all the way
through, taking fifteen minutes or more to hang it out
on a line in the dark bedroom air. But Vivian's fingers
were like an impatient spider inside his palm, and as
the story progressed he became more aware of her than
of the story people.

"—an old witch lived in this black castle—"

Vivian's lips kissed him on the cheek. It was like all
her kisses. It was like kisses before bodies were invented. Bodies are invented around about the age of
twelve or thirteen. Before that there are only sweet lips
and sweet kisses. There is a sweet something about
such kisses you never find again after someone puts a
body under your head.

Chris didn't have a body yet. Just his face. And, like
every time Vivian had ever kissed him, he responded.
After all, it was fun and it was as good as eating and
sleeping and playing all kinds of games. Her lips were
like a subtle sugar, and nothing else. For the past four
years since he was eight, every time he met Vivian and
that was usually once every month, because she lived

on the far side of town, there would be ghost stories and kisses and subtle sugar.

"—well, this witch in this castle—"

She kissed him on the lips, momentarily crumbling the castle. About ten seconds later he had to build it up again.

"—this witch in this castle had a beautiful young daughter named Helga. Helga lived in a dungeon and was treated very poorly by her evil old mother. She was very pretty and—"

The lips returned. This time for a longer stay.

"Go on with the story," said Leo.

"Yeah, hurry up," said Shirley, perturbed.

"—Ah," said Chris, breaking away a little, his breath a bit funny. "—One day the girl escaped from the dungeon and ran out into the woods, and the witch shouted after her—"

From there on the story got slower and slower, and wandered off in aimless, vague, and blundering directions. Vivian pressed close to him, kissing and breathing on his cheek as he told the halting tale. Then, very slowly, and with an architect's wonderful ability, she began to build his body for him! The Lord said ribs and there were ribs. The Lord said stomach and there was stomach! The Lord said legs and there were legs! The Lord said something else and there was something else!

It was funny finding his body under him so suddenly. For twelve years it had never been there. It was a pendulum under a clock, that body, and now Vivian

was setting it in motion, touching, urging, rocking it to
and fro, until it swung in dizzy warm arcs under the
machinery of the head. The clock was now running. A
clock cannot run until the pendulum moves. The clock
can be whole, ready, and intact and healthy, but until
that pendulum is thrust into motion there is nothing
but machinery without use.

"—and the girl ran out into the woods—"

"Hurry up, hurry up, Chris!" criticized Leo.

It was like the story of the thing coming up the
stairs, one by one, one by one. This whole evening,
here, now, in the dark. But—different.

Vivian's fingers deftly plucked at the belt buckle
and drew the metal tongue out, loosening it open.

Now she's at the first button.

Now she's at the second button.

So *like* that old story. But this was a *real* story.

"—so this girl ran into the woods—"

"You said that before, Chris," said Leo.

Now she's at the third button.

Now she's moved down to the fourth button, oh
God, and now to the fifth button, and now—

The same words that ended that *other* story, the *very
same two words*, but this time shouted passionately, inside, silently, silently, to yourself!

The two words!

The same two words used at the end of the story
about the thing coming up the stairs. The same two
words at the end!

Chris' voice didn't belong to him anymore:

"—and she ran into something, there was something, there was, well, anyway, this, she . . . well, she tried . . . er, someone chased her . . . or . . . well, she ran, anyway, and she came, down she went and she ran and then, and then, she—"

Vivian moved against him. Her lips sealed up that story inside him and wouldn't let it out. The castle fell thundering for the last time into ruin, in a burst of blazing flame, and there was nothing in the world but this newly invented body of his and the fact that a girl's body is not so much land, like the hills of Wisconsin, pretty to look at. Here was all the beauty and singing and firelight and warmth in the world. Here was the meaning of all change and all movement and all adjustment.

Far away in the dim hushed lands below a phone rang. It was so faint it was like one of those voices crying in a forgotten dungeon. A phone rang and Chris could hear nothing.

It seemed there was a faint, halfhearted criticism from Leo and Shirley, and then a few minutes later, Chris realized that Leo and Shirley were clumsily kissing one another, and nothing else, just clumsily adjusting faces to one another. The room was silent. The stories were told and all of space engulfed the room.

It was so strange. Chris could only lie there and let Vivian tell him all of it with this dark, unbelievable pantomime. You are not told all of your life of things like this, he thought. You are not told at all. Maybe it is too good to tell, too strange and wonderful to give words about.

Footsteps came up the stairs. Very slow, very sad footsteps this time. Very slow and soft.

"Quick!" whispered Vivian. She pulled away, smoothing her dress. Like a blind man, fingerless, Chris fumbled with his belt buckle and buttons. "Quick!" whispered Vivian.

She flicked the light on and the world shocked Chris with its unreality. Blank walls staring, wide and senseless after the dark; lovely, soft, moving, and secretive dark. And as the footsteps advanced up the stairs, the four of them were once again solemn ramrods against the wall, and Vivian was retelling her story:

"—now he's at the top stair—"

The door opened. Auntie stood there, tears on her face. That was enough in itself to tell, to give the message.

"We just received a call from the hospital," she said. "Your Uncle Lester passed away a few minutes ago."

They sat there.

"You'd better come downstairs," said Auntie.

They arose slowly. Chris felt drunk and unsteady and warm. He waited for Auntie to go out and the others to follow. He came last of all, down into the hushed land of weeping and solemn tightened faces.

As he descended the last step he couldn't help but feel a strange thing moving in his mind. Oh, Uncle Lester, they've taken your body away from you, and I've got *mine,* and it isn't fair! Oh, it isn't fair, because this is *so good!*

In a few minutes they would go home. The silent house would hold their weeping a few days, the radio would be snapped off for a week, and laughter would come and be throttled in birth.

He began to cry.

Mother looked at him. Uncle Inar looked at him and some of the others looked at him. Vivian, too. And Leo, so big and solemn standing there.

Chris was crying and everybody looked.

But only Vivian knew that he was crying for joy, a warm good crying of a child who has found treasure buried deep and warm in his very body.

"Oh, Chris," said Mother, and came to comfort him. "There, there."

Grand Theft

Emily Wilkes had her eyes pried open by a peculiar sound at three o'clock in the deep morning, with no moon, and only the stars as witness.

"Rose?" she said.

Her sister, in a separate bed not three feet away, already had her eyes wide, so was not surprised.

"You *hear* it?" she said, spoiling everything.

"I was going to tell *you*," said Emily. "Since you already seem to know, there's no use—"

She stopped and sat up in bed, as did Rose, both pulled by invisible wires. They sat there, two ancient sisters, one eighty, the other eighty-one, both bone-thin and bundles of nerves because they were staring at the ceiling.

Emily Wilkes nodded her head up. "*That* what you heard?"

"Mice in the attic?"

"Sounds bigger'n that. Rats."

"Yes, but it sounds like they're wearing boots and carrying bags."

That did it. Out of bed, they grabbed their wrappers and went downstairs as fast as arthritis would allow. No one wanted to stay underneath whoever wore those boots.

Below they grabbed the banister and stared up, whispering.

"What would anyone do in our attic *this* time of night?"

"Burgling all our old junk?"

"You don't think they'll come down and *attack* us?"

"What, two old fools, with skinny backsides?"

"Thank God, the trapdoor only works one way, and is locked beneath."

They began to edge step by step back up toward the hidden sounds.

"I *know!*" said Rose, suddenly. "In the Chicago papers last week: they're stealing *antique furniture!*"

"Pshaw! We're the only antiques here!"

"Still, there's some up there. A Morris chair, that's old. Some dining room chairs, older, and a cut crystal chandelier."

"From the dime store, 1914. So ugly we couldn't put it out with the trash. Listen."

It was quieter above. On the top floor, they gazed at the ceiling trapdoor and cocked their ears.

"Someone's opening my trunk." Emily clapped her hands to her mouth. "Hear that? The hinges need oiling."

"Why would they open your trunk? Nothing is there."

"Maybe *something* . . ."

Above, in the dark, the trunk lid fell.

"Fool!" whispered Emily.

Someone tiptoed across the attic floor, careful after being clumsy.

"There's a window up there, they're climbing out!"

The two sisters ran to their own bedroom window.

"Unlock the screen, poke your head out!" cried Rose.

"And let them *see* me? No, ma'am!"

They waited and heard a scraping noise and a clatter as something fell on the driveway below.

Gasping, they shoved the screen out to peer down and see a long ladder being toted along the driveway by two shadows. One of the shadows grasped a small white packet in his free hand.

"They stole something!" hissed Emily. "Come!"

Downstairs, they threw the front door wide to see two sets of footprints on the lawn in the dew. A truck, at the curb, pulled away.

Running out, both ladies shaded their eyes to read the vanishing license plate.

"Damnation!" cried Emily. "Did you *see*?"

"A seven and nine, is all. Do we call the police?"

"Not till we know what's *gone*. Shake a leg."

By flashlight on the attic stairs they unlocked the trapdoor and climbed up into darkness.

Emily swept the attic room with the flash as they

stumbled through old suitcases, a child's bike, and that truly ugly chandelier.

"Nothing's gone," said Rose. "Odd-peculiar."

"Maybe. Here's the trunk. Grab on."

As they lifted, the lid sprang back with an exhalation of dust and ancient scent.

"My God, remember *that?* Ben Hur perfume, 1925, came out with the movie!"

"Hush," said Emily. "Oh, hush!"

She poked the flashlight into an empty place in the middle of an old party dress: a sort of crushed pocket, two inches deep, four inches wide, and eight inches long.

"Dear God in heaven!" cried Emily. "They're gone!"

"Gone?"

"My love letters! From 1919 and 1920 and 1921! Wrapped in a pink ribbon, thirty of them. Gone!"

Emily stared down at the coffin-shaped emptiness in the middle of the old party dress. "Why would anyone steal love letters written so far back by someone probably dead to someone, me, good as dead?"

"Emily Bernice!" exclaimed Rose. "Where you been lately? You ever see those TV matinees make you want your mouth washed out with soap? How about the gossip columns in the town gazette? You ever look at the crazy ladies' magazines at the beauty parlor?"

"I try *not* to."

"Next time, look! All those folks got up on the dark side of the bed. Our phone'll ring tomorrow. Whoever stole your letters'll want cash to hand them back, or edit them for some crazed women's book club, or for advice in a lovelorn column. Blackmail. What else? Publicity! Come on!"

"Don't call the police! Oh, Rose, I won't wash my underwear for them or anyone! Is there any grape wine left in the pantry? Rose, move! It's the end of the world!"

Going down, they almost fell.

The next day every time a special-delivery mail truck ran by, Emily would part the parlor curtains and wait for it to stop. It never did.

The day after, when a TV repair van slowed to seek an address, Emily stepped out to fend off any ill-mannered reporters who might nose in. They never nosed.

On the third day, when intuition said there had been time enough for the *Green Town Gazette* to save up its spit and let fly, the spit was not saved or flown.

But . . .

On the fourth day a single letter fell in her mailbox with no mailman in sight. Emily's name on the letter seemed written in lemon juice and scorched to raise the calligraphy.

"Look," Emily whispered, "Emily Bernice *Watriss!* And the two-cent stamp is canceled: June fourth, 1921." She held the letter up to X-ray its mystery. "Whoever stole this four nights ago," she gasped, "is sending it *back* to me! Why?"

"Open it," said Rose. "The outside is sixty-two years old. What's *inside?*"

Emily took a deep breath and slid out the brittle paper with brownish handwriting in a fine flourished Palmer penmanship.

"June fourth, 1921," she read. "And the letter says: My dearest dear Emily—"

Emily let a tear drop from one eye.

"Well, go *on!*" said Rose.

"It's *my* love letter!"

"I know, I know, but we're two old battle-axes now. Nothing can offend us! Gimme that!"

Rose grabbed and turned the letter toward the light. Her voice faded as her eyes squinted along the fine calligraphy from another year:

"My dearest dear Emily: I know not how to pour out all that is in my heart. I have admired you for so many years and yet, when we have danced or shared picnics at the lake, I have been unable to speak. At home I stare at myself in the mirror and hate my cowardice. But now at last I must speak my tenderest thoughts or go mad beyond salvation. I fear to offend, and this small letter will take many hours to rewrite. Dear, dear Emily, know my affection and willingness to share some part of my life near or with you. If you could look upon me with the smallest kindness, I would be overcome with happiness. I have had to stop myself from touching your hand. And the thought of anything more, the merest kiss, shakes me that I even dare to say these words. My intentions are honorable. If you would permit, I would like to speak to your parents. Until that hour and day, I send you my affections and kindest thoughts for your future life and existence."

Rose's voice sounded clearly with these last words . . .

"Signed William Ross Fielding."

Rose glanced at Emily. "William Ross Fielding? Who was *he*, writing to you and madly in love?"

"Oh, God," Emily Bernice Watriss cried, her eyes blind with tears. "I'll be damned if *I* know!"

Day after day the letters arrived, not by mail, but slipped in the box at midnight or dawn to be read aloud by Rose or Emily who took turns wiping their eyes. Day after day the writer from a far year begged Emily's pardon, worried on her future, and signed himself with a flourish and an almost audible sigh, William Ross Fielding.

And each day Emily, eyes shut, said, "Read it again. I *almost* got a face to match the words!"

By week's end, with six ancient letters stacked and crumbling fast, Emily fell into exhaustion and exclaimed, "Stop! Devil take that sinful blackmailer who won't show his face! Burn it!"

"Not yet," said Rose, arriving with no ancient yellowed note, but a spanking bright new envelope, nameless outside, nameless in.

Emily, back from the dead, snatched it and read:

"I am ashamed for assisting all this trouble which now must stop. You can find your mail at 11 South St. James. Forgive."

And no signature.

"I don't understand," Emily said.

"Easy as pie," said Rose. "Whoever's sending your letters back is making affectionate approaches with someone else's notes from when Coolidge was president!"

"My God, Rose, feel my face: red-hot. Why would someone climb a ladder, rob an attic, and run? Why not stand on our lawn and yell?"

"Because," said Rose, quietly, turning the new letter over, "maybe whoever wrote this is just as shy now as William Ross Fielding was way back where you can't remember. Now what?"

"I wonder . . ." Emily stared out the window. ". . . who lives at 11 South St. James."

"Here it is."

They stood in front of it late in the day.

11 South St. James.

"Who's there looking out at us this very minute?" said Emily.

"Not the gent who sent you the confession," said Rose. "He just helped carry the ladder but can't carry the guilt. In there now is the mad fool who's been sending your notes. And if we don't move the whole street'll be a beehive. Shake a leg."

They crossed the porch and rang the bell. The front door drifted wide. An old man, well into his late seventies, stood there, astonished.

"Why, Emily Bernice Watriss," he exclaimed. "Hello!"

"What," said Emily Bernice Watriss, "in hell's name are you *up* to?"

"Right now?" he said. "Tea's ready. Yes?"

They sidled in, perched themselves, ready to run, and watched him pour teakettle water over some orange pekoe leaves.

"Cream or lemon?" he asked.

"Don't cream and lemon me!" Emily said.

"Please."

They took their cups but said nothing and drank none, as he sipped his own and said:

"My friend called to admit he had revealed my address. This whole week has made me incredibly sad."

"How do you think *I* feel?" Emily exclaimed. "You *are* the one, then, who stole my mail and sent it back?"

"I am that one, yes."

"Well then, make your demands!"

"Demands? No, no! Did you fear blackmail? How stupid of me not to guess you might think so. No, no. Are those the letters there?"

"They are!"

"The letter on the top, the first one, dated June fourth, 1921. Would you mind opening it? Just hold it where I can't read it, and let me speak, yes?"

Emily fumbled the letter out on her lap.

"Well?" she said.

"Just this," he said, and shut his eyes and began to recite in a voice they could hardly hear:

"My dearest dear Emily—"

Emily sucked in her breath.

The old man waited, eyes shut, and then repeated the words signed across the inside of his eyelids:

"My dearest dear Emily. I know not how to address you or pour out all that is in my heart—"

Emily let her breath out.

The old man whispered:

"—I have admired you for so many months and years, and yet when I have seen you, when we have danced or shared picnics with your friends at the lake, I had found myself unable to speak—but now at last I must speak my tenderest thoughts or find myself mad beyond salvation—"

Rose took out her handkerchief and applied it to her nose. Emily took out hers and applied it to her eyes.

His voice was soft and then loud and then soft again:

"—and the thought of anything more than that, the merest kiss, shakes me that I dare to put it in words—"

He finished, whispering:

"—until that hour and day, I send you my affections and kindest thoughts for your future life and existence. Signed William Ross Fielding. Now. Second letter."

Emily opened the second letter and held it where he could not see it.

"Dearest dear one," he said. "You have not answered my first letter which means one or several things: you did not receive it, it was kept from you, or you received, destroyed it, or hid it away. If I have offended you, forgive— Everywhere I go, your name is spoken. Young men speak of you. Young women tell rumors that soon you may travel away by ocean liner . . ."

"They did that, in those days," said Emily, almost

to herself. "Young women, sometimes young men, sent off for a year to forget."

"Even if there was nothing *to* forget?" said the old man, reading his own palms spread out on his knees.

"Even that. I have another letter here. Can you tell me what it says?"

She opened it and her eyes grew wet as she read the lines and heard him, head down, speak them quietly, from remembrance.

"Dearest dear, do I dare say it, love of my life? You are leaving tomorrow and will not return until long after Christmas. Your engagement has been announced to someone already in Paris, waiting. I wish you a grand life and a happy one and many children. Forget my name. Forget it? Why, dear girl, you never knew it. Willie or Will? I think you called me that. But there was no last name, really, so nothing to forget. Remember instead my love. Signed W.R.F."

Finished, he sat back and opened his eyes as she folded the letter and placed it with the others in her lap, tears running down her cheeks.

"Why," she asked at last, "did you steal the letters? And use them this way, sixty years later? Who told you where the letters might be? I buried them in that coffin, that trunk, when I sailed to France. I don't think I have looked at them more than once in the past thirty years. Did William Ross Fielding tell you about them?"

"Why, dear girl, haven't you guessed?" said the old man. "My Lord, I *am* William Ross Fielding."

There was an incredibly long silence.

"Let me look at you." Emily leaned forward as he raised his head into the light.

"No," she said. "I wish I could say. Nothing."

"It's an old man's face now," he said. "No matter. When you sailed around the world one way, I went another. I have lived in many countries and done many things, a bachelor traveling. When I heard that you had no children and that your husband died, many years ago, I drifted back to this, my grandparents' house. It has taken all these years to nerve myself to find and send this best part of my life to you."

The two sisters were very still. You could almost hear their hearts beating. The old man said:

"What now?"

"Why," said Emily Bernice Watriss Wilkes slowly, "every day for the next two weeks, send the rest of the letters. One by one."

He looked at her, steadily.

"And then?" he said.

"Oh, God!" she said. "I don't know. Let's see."

"Yes, yes. Indeed. Let's say good-bye."

Opening the front door he almost touched her hand.

"My dear dearest Emily," he said.

"Yes?" She waited.

"What—" he said.

"Yes?" she said.

"What . . ." he said, and swallowed. "What . . . are you . . ."

She waited.

"Doing tonight?" he finished, quickly.

Remember Me?

"**R**emember me? Of course, surely you *do!*"
His hand extended, the stranger waited.

"Why, yes," I said. "You're—"

I stopped and searched around for help. We were
in middle-street in Florence, Italy, at high noon. He had
been rushing one way, I the other, and almost collided.
Now he waited to hear his name off my lips. Panicking,
I rummaged my brain which ran on empty.

"You're—" I said again.

He seized my hand as if fearing I might bolt and
run. His face was a sunburst. He *knew* me! Shouldn't I
return the honor? There's a good dog, he thought,
speak!

"I'm Harry!" he cried.

"Harry . . . ?"

"Stadler!" he barked with a laugh. "Your butcher!"

"Jesus, of course. Harry, you old son of a bitch!" I
pumped his hand with relief.

He almost danced with joy. "*That* son of a bitch, yes! Nine thousand miles from home. No wonder you didn't know me! Hey, we'll get killed out here. I'm at the Grand Hotel. The lobby parquetry floor, amazing! Dinner tonight? Florentine steaks—listen to your butcher, eh? Seven tonight! Yes!"

I opened my mouth to suck and blow out in a great refusal, but—

"Tonight!" he cried.

He spun about and ran, almost plowed under by a bumblebee motorbike. At the far curb he yelled:

"Harry Stadler!"

"Leonard Douglas," I shouted, inanely.

"I know." He waved and vanished in the mob. "I know . . ."

My God! I thought, staring at my massaged and abandoned hand. Who *was* that?

My butcher.

Now I saw him at his counter grinding hamburger, a tiny white toy-boat cap capsizing on his thin blond hair, Germanic, imperturbable, his cheeks all pork sausage as he pounded a steak into submission.

My butcher, *yes!*

"Jesus!" I muttered for the rest of the day. "Christ! What made me accept? Why in hell did he *ask?* We don't even *know* each other, except when he says, That's five bucks sixty, and I say, So long! Hell!"

I rang his hotel room every half hour all afternoon. No answer.

"Will you leave a message, sir?"

"No thanks."

Coward, I thought. Leave a message: sick. Leave a message: died!

I stared at the phone, helpless. Of course I hadn't recognized him. Whoever recognizes anyone away from their counter, desk, car, piano, or wherever someone stands, sits, sells, speaks, provides, or dispenses? The mechanic free of his grease-monkey jumpsuit, the lawyer devoid of his pinstripes and wearing a fiery hibiscus sport shirt, the club woman released from her corset and crammed in an explosive bikini—all, all unfamiliar, strange, easily insulted if unrecognized! We all expect that no matter where we go or dress, we will be instantly recognized. Like disguised MacArthurs we stride ashore in far countries crying: "*I* have returned!"

But does anyone *give* a damn? This butcher, now—minus his cap, without the blood-fingerprinted smock, without the fan whirling above his head to drive off flies, without bright knives, sharp tenterhooks, whirled bologna slicers, mounds of pink flesh or spreads of marbled beef, he was the masked avenger.

Besides, travel had freshened him. Travel does that. Two weeks of luscious foods, rare wines, long sleeps, wondrous architectures and a man wakes ten years younger to hate going home to be old.

Myself? I was at the absolute peak of losing years in gaining miles. My butcher and I had become quasi-teenagers reborn to collide in Florentine traffic to gibber and paw each other's memories.

"Damn it to hell!" I jabbed his number on the touch-phone, viciously. Five o'clock: silence. Six: no answer. Seven: the same. Christ!

"Stop!" I yelled out the window.

All of Florence's church bells sounded, sealing my doom.

Bang! Someone slammed a door, on their way out. Me.

When we met at five minutes after seven, we were like two angry lovers who hadn't seen each other for days and now rushed in a turmoil of self-pity toward a supper with killed appetites.

Eat and run, no, eat and flee, was in our faces as we swayed in mid-lobby, at the last moment seized each other's hands. Might we arm-wrestle? From somewhere crept false smiles and tepid laughter.

"Leonard Douglas," he cried, "you old son of a bitch!"

He stopped, red-faced. Butchers, after all, do not swear at old customers!

"I mean," he said, "come *on!*"

He shoved me into the elevator and babbled all the way up to the penthouse restaurant.

"What a coincidence. Middle of the street. Fine food here. Here's our floor. Out!"

We sat to dine.

"Wine for me." The butcher eyed the wine list, like an old friend. "Here's a swell one. 1970, St. Emilion. Yes?"

"Thanks. A very dry vodka martini."

My butcher scowled.

"But," I said, quickly, "I *will* have some wine, of course!"

I ordered salad to start. He scowled again.

"The salad and the martini will ruin your taste for the wine. Beg pardon."

"Well then," I said, hastily, "the salad, *later*."

We ordered our steaks, his rare, mine well-done.

"Sorry," said my butcher, "but you *should* treat your meat more kindly."

"Not like St. Joan, eh?" I said, and laughed.

"That's a good one. Not like St. Joan."

At which moment the wine arrived to be uncorked. I offered my glass quickly and, glad that my martini had been delayed, or might never come, made the next minute easier by sniffing, whirling, and sipping the St. Emilion. My butcher watched, as a cat might watch a rather strange dog.

I swallowed the merest sip, eyes closed, and nodded.

The stranger across the table also sipped and nodded.

A tie.

We stared at the twilight horizon of Florence.

"Well . . ." I said, frantic for conversation ". . . what do you think of Florence's art?"

"Paintings make me nervous," he admitted. "What I *really* like is walking around. Italian women! I'd like to ice-pack and ship them home!"

"Er, yes . . ." I cleared my throat. "But Giotto . . . ?"

"Giotto bores me. Sorry. He's too soon in art history for me. Stick figures. Masaccio's better. Raphael's best. And *Rubens!* I have a butcher's taste for flesh."

"Rubens?"

"Rubens!" Harry Stadler forked some neat little salami slices, popped them in his mouth, and chewed opinions. "Rubens! All bosom and bum, big cumulus clouds of pink flesh, eh? You can feel the heart beating like a kettledrum in a ton of that stuff. Every woman a bed; throw yourself on them, sink from sight. To hell with the boy David, all that cold white marble and no fig leaf! No, no, I like color, life, and meat that covers the bone. You're not *eating!*"

"Watch." I ate my bloody salami and pink bologna and my dead white provolone, wondering if I should ask his opinion of the cold white colorless cheeses of the world.

The headwaiter delivered our steaks.

Stadler's was so rare you could run blood tests on it. Mine resembled a withered black man's head left to smoke and char my plate.

My butcher growled at my burnt offering.

"My God," he cried, "they treated Joan of Arc better than that! Will you puff it or chew it?"

"But yours," I laughed, "is still *breathing!*"

My steak sounded like crunched autumn leaves, every time I chewed.

Stadler, like W. C. Fields, hacked his way through a wall of living flesh, dragging his canoe behind him.

He killed his dinner. I buried mine.

We ate swiftly. All too soon, in a shared panic, we sensed that we must talk once more.

We ate in a terrible silence like an old married couple, angry at lost arguments, the reasons for which were also lost, leaving irritability and muted rage.

We buttered bread to fill the silence. We ordered coffee, which filled more time and at last settled back, watching that other stranger across a snowfield of linen, napery, and silver. Then, abomination of abominations, I heard myself say:

"When we get home, we must have dinner some night to talk about our time here, yes? Florence, the weather, the paintings."

"Yes." He downed his drink. *"No!"*

"What?"

"No," he said, simply. "Let's face it, Leonard, when we were home we had nothing in common. Even here we have nothing except time, distance, and travel to share. We have no talk, no interests. Hell, it's a shame, but there it is. This whole thing was impulsive, for the best, or at the worst, mysterious reasons. You're alone, I'm alone in a strange city at noon, and here tonight. But we're like a couple of grave-diggers who meet and try to shake hands, but their ectoplasm falls right through each other, hmm? We've kidded ourselves all day."

I sat there stunned. I shut my eyes, felt as if I might be angry, then gave a great gusting exhalation.

"You're the most honest man I've ever known."

"I hate being honest and realistic." Then he laughed. "I tried to call you all afternoon."

"I tried to call *you!*"

"I wanted to cancel dinner."

"Me, too!"

"I never got through."

"I missed *you.*"

"My God!"

"Jesus Christ!"

We both began to laugh, threw our heads back, and almost fell from our chairs.

"This is *rich!*"

"It most certainly *is!*" I said, imitating Oliver Hardy's way of speaking.

"God, order another bottle of champagne!"

"Waiter!"

We hardly stopped laughing as the waiter poured the second bottle.

"Well, we have *one* thing in common," said Harry Stadler.

"What's that?"

"This whole cockamamie silly stupid wonderful day, starting at noon, ending here. We'll tell this story to friends the rest of our lives. How I invited you, and you fell in with it not wanting to, and how we both tried to call it off before it started, and how we both came to dinner hating it, and how we blurted it out, silly, silly, and how suddenly—" He stopped. His eyes watered and his voice softened. "How suddenly it wasn't so silly anymore. But okay. Suddenly we liked each other in our foolishness. And if we don't try to make the rest of the evening too long, it won't be so bad, after all."

I tapped my champagne glass to his. The tenderness had reached me, too, along with the stupid and silly.

"We won't ever have any dinners back home."

"No."

"And we don't have to be afraid of long talks about nothing."

"Just the weather for a few seconds, now and then."

"And we won't meet socially."

"Here's to that."

"But suddenly it's a nice night, old Leonard Douglas, customer of mine."

"Here's to Harry Stadler." I raised my glass. "Wherever he goes from here."

"Bless me. Bless you."

We drank and simply sat there for another five minutes, warm and comfortable as old friends who had suddenly found that a long long time ago we had loved the same beautiful librarian who had touched our books and touched our cheeks. But the memory was fading.

"It's going to rain." I arose with my wallet.

Stadler stared until I put the wallet back in my jacket.

"Thanks and good night."

"Thanks to you," he said, "I'm not so lonely now, no matter what."

I gulped the rest of my wine, gasped with pleasure, ruffled Stadler's hair with a quick hand, and ran.

At the door I turned. He saw this and shouted across the room.

"*Remember* me?"

I pretended to pause, scratch my head, cudgel my memory. Then I pointed at him and cried:

"The butcher!"

He lifted his drink.

"Yes!" he called. "The butcher!"

I hurried downstairs and across the parquetry floor which was too beautiful to walk on, and out into a storm.

I walked in the rain for a long while, face up.

Hell, I thought, I don't feel so lonely *myself!*

Then, soaked through, and laughing, I ducked and ran all the way back to my hotel.

Fee Fie Foe Fum

T he postman came melting along the sidewalk in the hot summer sun, his nose dripping, his fingers wet on his full leather pouch. "Let's see. Next house is Barton's. Three letters. One for Thomas Q., one for his wife, Liddy, and one for old Grandma. Is *she* still alive? How they *do* hang on."

He slid the letters in the box and froze.

A lion roared.

He stepped back, eyes wide.

The screen door sang open on its taut spring. "Morning, Ralph."

"Morning, Mrs. Barton. Just heard your pet lion."

"What?"

"Lion. In your kitchen."

She listened. "Oh, *that?* Our Garburator. You know: garbage disposal unit."

"Your husband buy it?"

"Right. You men and your machines. That thing'll eat anything, bones and all."

"Careful. It might eat you."

"No. I'm a lion-tamer." She laughed, and listened. "Hey, it *does* sound like a lion."

"A hungry one. Well, so long."

He drifted off into the hot morning.

Liddy ran upstairs with the letters.

"Grandma?" She tapped on a door. "Letter for you."

The door was silent.

"Grandma? You in there?"

After a long pause, a dry-wicker voice replied, "Yep."

"What're you doing?"

"Ask me no questions, I'll tell you no lies," chanted the old one, hid away.

"You've been in there all morning."

"I might be here all year," snapped Grandma.

Liddy tried the knob. "You've locked the door."

"Well, so I *have!*"

"You coming down to lunch, Grandma?"

"Nope. Nor supper. I won't come down till you throw that damned machine out of the kitchen." Her flinty eye jittered in the keyhole, staring out at her granddaughter.

"You mean the Garburator?" Liddy smiled.

"I heard the postman. He's right. I won't have a lion in *my* house! *Listen!* There's your husband now, *using* it."

Below stairs, the Garburator roared, swallowing garbage, bones and all.

"Liddy!" her husband called. "Liddy, come on down. See it work!"

Liddy spoke to Grandma's keyhole. "Don't you want to watch, Grandma?"

"Nope!"

Footsteps arose behind Liddy. Turning, she found Tom on the top stairs. "Go down and try, Liddy. I got some extra bones from the butcher. It really *chews* them."

She descended toward the kitchen. "It's grisly, but heck, why not?"

Thomas Barton stood neat and alone at Grandma's door and waited a full minute, motionless, a prim smile on his lips. He knocked softly, delicately. "Grandma?" he whispered. No reply. He patted the knob tenderly. "I know you're there, you old ruin. Grandma, you *hear?* Down below. You *hear?* How come your door's locked? Something wrong? What could bother you on such a nice summer day?"

Silence. He moved into the bathroom.

The hall stood empty. From the bath came sounds of water running. Then, Thomas Barton's voice, full and resonant in the tile room, sang:

"Fee fie foe fum
I smell the blood of an Englishmum;
Be she alive or be she dead,
I'll gurrrr-innnnnnd *her bones to make my bread!"*

In the kitchen, the lion roared.

Grandma smelled like attic furniture, smelled like

dust, smelled like a lemon, and resembled a withered flower. Her firm jaw sagged and her pale gold eyes were flinty bright as she sat in her chair like a hatchet, cleaving the hot noon air, rocking.

She heard Thomas Barton's song.

Her heart grew an ice crystal.

She had heard her grandson-in-law rip open the crate this morning, like a child with an evil Christmas toy. The fierce cracklings and tearings, the cry of triumph, the eager fumbling of his hands over the toothy machine. He had caught Grandma's yellow eagle eye in the hall entry and given her a mighty wink. Bang! She had run to slam her door!

Grandma shivered in her room all day.

Liddy knocked again, concerning lunch, but was scolded away.

Through the simmering afternoon, the Garburator lived gloriously in the kitchen sink. It fed, it ate, it made grinding, smacking noises with hungry mouth and vicious hidden teeth. It whirled, it groaned. It ate pig knuckles, coffee grounds, eggshells, drumsticks. It was an ancient hunger which, unfed, waited, crouched, metal entrail upon metal entrail, little flailing propellers of razor-screw all bright with lust.

Liddy carried supper up on a tray.

"Slide it under the door," shouted Grandma.

"Heavens!" said Liddy. "Open the door long enough for me to poke it in at you."

"Look over your shoulder; anyone *lurking* in the hall?"

"No."

"So!" The door flew wide. Half the corn was spilled being yanked in. She gave Liddy a shove and slammed the door. "That was close!" she cried, holding the rabbit-run in her bosom.

"Grandma, what's got *in* you?"

Grandma watched the knob twist. "No use telling, you wouldn't believe, child. Out of the goodness of my heart I moved you here a year ago. Tom and I always spit at each other. Now he wants me gone, but he won't get *me*, no sir! I know his trick. One day you'll come from the store and I'll be nowhere. You'll ask Tom: What happened to old Grandma? Sweet-smiling, he'll say: Grandma? Just now decided to hike to Illinois! Just packed and *left!* And you won't see Grandma again, Liddy, you know why, you got an inkling?"

"Grandma, that's gibberish. Tom *loves* you!"

"Loves my house, my antiques, my mattress-money, *that's* what he loves dearly! Get away, I'll work this out myself! I'm locked in here till hell burns out."

"What about your canary, Grandma?"

"*You* feed Singing Sam! Buy hamburger for Spottie, he's a happy dog, I can't let him starve. Bring Kitten up on occasion, I can't live without cats. Now, shoo! I'm climbing in bed."

Grandma put herself to bed like a corpse preparing its own coffin. She folded her yellow wax fingers on her ruffly bosom, as her mothlike eyelids winced shut. What to do? What weapon to use against that clockwork mechanic? Liddy? But Liddy was fresh as new-baked bread, her rosy face was excited only by cinnamon buns and raised muffins, she smelled of yeast and warm milk. The only murder Liddy might consider was one where the victim ended on the dinner platter, orange sucked in mouth, cloves in pink hide, silent under the knife. No, you couldn't tell wild truths to Liddy, she'd only laugh and bake another cake.

Grandma sighed a lost sigh.

The small vein in her chicken neck stopped throbbing. Only the fragile bellows of her tiny lungs moved in the room like the ghost of an apprehension, whispering.

Below, in its bright chromed cage, the lion slept.

A week passed.

Only "heading for the bathroom" ran Grandma out of hiding. When Thomas Barton throttled his car she panicked from her bedroom. Her bathroom visits were frantic and explosive. She fell back in bed a few minutes later. Some mornings, Thomas delayed going to his office, purposely, and stood, erect as a numeral one, mathematically clean, working on her door with his eyes, smiling at this delay.

Once in the middle of a summer night, she sneaked down and fed the "lion" a bag of nuts and bolts. She trusted Liddy to turn on the beast at dawn and choke it to death. She lay in bed early, hearing the first stirs and yawns of the two arising people, waiting for the sound of the lion shrieking, choked by bolt, washer, and screw, dying of indigestible parts.

She heard Thomas walk downstairs.

Half an hour later his voice said, "Here's a present for you, Grandma. My lion says: No thanks."

Peeking out, later, she found the nuts and bolts laid in a neat row on her sill.

On the morning of the twelfth day of imprisonment, Grandma dialed her bedroom phone:

"Hello, Tom, that *you*? You at *work*, Tom?"

"This is my office number, *why*?"

"True." She hung up and tiptoed down the hall stairs into the parlor.

Liddy looked up, shocked. "Grandma!"

"Who else?" snapped the old one. "Tom here?"

"You *know* he's working."

"Yes, yes!" Grandma stared unblinkingly about, gumming her porcelain teeth. "Just phoned him. Take ten minutes for him to drive home, don't it?"

"Sometimes half an hour."

"Good." Grandma mourned. "Can't stay in my room. Just had to come down, see you, set awhile, breathe." She pulled a tiny gold watch from her bosom. "In ten minutes, back up I go. I'll phone Tom then, to see if he's still at work. I might come down again, if he is." She opened the front door and called out into the fresh summer day. "Spottie, here, Spot! Kitten, here, Kitt!"

A large white dog, unmarked, appeared, yelping, to be let in, followed by a plump black cat which leaped in her lap when she sat.

"Good pals," Grandma cooed, stroking them. She

lay back, eyes shut, and listened for the song of her wonderful canary in his golden cage in the dining room bay window.

Silence.

Grandma rose and peeked through the dining room door.

It was an instant before she realized what had happened to the cage.

It was empty.

"Singing Sam's gone!" screamed Grandma. She ran to dump the cage upside down. "Gone!"

The cage fell to the floor, just as Liddy appeared. "I thought it was quiet, but didn't know why. I must've left the cage open by mistake—"

"You *sure?* Oh my God, *wait!*"

Grandma closed her eyes and groped her way out to the kitchen. Finding the kitchen sink cool under her fingers, she opened her eyes and looked down.

The Garburator lay gleaming, silent, its mouth wide. At its rim lay a small yellow feather.

Grandma turned on the water.

The Garburator made a chewing, swallowing noise.

Slowly, Grandma clamped both skinny hands over her mouth.

Her room was quiet as a pool; she remained in it like a quiet forest thing, knowing that once out of its shade, she might be set on by a jungle terror. With Singing Sam's disappearance, the horror had made a mushroom growth into hysteria. Liddy had had to fight her away from the sink, where Grandma was trying to bat the gluttonous machine with a hammer. Liddy had forced her upstairs to put ice compresses on her raging brow.

"Singing Sam, he's killed poor Sam!" Grandma had sobbed and wailed. But then the thrashing ceased, firm resolve seeped back. She locked Liddy out again and now there was a cold rage in her, in company with the fear and trembling; to think Tom would *dare* do this to her!

Now she would not open the door far enough to allow even supper in on a tray. She had dinner rattled to a chair outside, and she ate through the door-crack, held open on a safety chain just far enough so you saw her skeleton hand dart out like a bird shadowing the meat and corn, flying off with morsels, flying back for more. "Thanks!" And the swift bird vanished behind the shut door.

"Singing Sam must've flown off, Grandma." Liddy phoned from the drugstore to Grandma's room, because Grandma refused to talk any other way.

"Good *night!*" cried Grandma, and disconnected.

The next day Grandma phoned Thomas again.

"You *there*, Tom?"

"Where *else?*" said Tom.

Grandma ran downstairs.

"Here, Spot, Spottie! Here, Kitten!"

The dog and cat did not answer.

She waited, gripping the door, and then she called for Liddy.

Liddy came.

"Liddy," said Grandma, in a stiff voice, barely audible, not looking at her. "Go look in the Garburator. Lift up the metal piece. Tell me what you see."

Grandma heard Liddy's footsteps far away. A silence.

"What do you see?" cried Grandma, impatient and afraid.

Liddy hesitated. "A piece of white fur—"

"Yes?"

"And—a piece of black fur."

"Stop. No more. Get me an aspirin."

Liddy obeyed. "You and Tom must stop, Grandma. This silly game, I mean. I'll chew him out tonight. It's not funny anymore. I thought if I let you alone, you'd stop raving about some lion. But now it's been a week—"

Grandma said, "Do you really think we'll ever see Spot or Kitten again?"

"They'll be home for supper, hungry as ever," Liddy replied. "It was crude of Tom to stuff that fur in the Garburator. I'll stop it."

"Will you, Liddy?" Grandma walked upstairs as in a trance. "Will you, really?"

Grandma lay planning through the night. This all must end. The dog and cat had not returned for supper, though Liddy laughed and said they would. Grandma nodded. She and Tom must tie a final knot now. Destroy the machine? But he'd install another, and, between them, put her into an asylum if she didn't stop babbling. No, a crisis must be forced, on her own grounds, in her own time and way. How? Liddy must be tricked from the house. Then Grandma must meet Thomas, at long last, alone. She was dead tired of his smiles, worn away by this quick eating and hiding, this lizard-darting in and out doors. No. She sniffed the cooling wind at midnight.

"Tomorrow," she decided, "will be a grand day for a picnic."

"Grandma!"

Liddy's voice through the keyhole. "We're leaving now. Sure you won't come along?"

"No, child! Enjoy yourselves. It's a fine morning!"

Bright Saturday. Grandma, early, had telephoned downstairs suggesting her two relatives take ham and pickle sandwiches out through the green forests. Tom had assented swiftly. Of course! A picnic! Tom had laughed and rubbed his hands.

"Good-bye, Grandma!"

The rustle of picnic wickers, the slamming door, the car purring off into the excellent weather.

"There." Grandma appeared in the living room. "Now it's just a matter of time. He'll sneak back. I could tell by his voice; *too* happy! He'll creep in, all alone, to visit."

75

She swept the house with a brisk straw broom. She felt she was sweeping out all the numerical bits and pieces of Thomas Barton, cleaning him away. All the tobacco fragments and neat newspapers he had flourished with his morning Brazilian coffee, clean threads from his scrupulous tweed suit, clips from his office supplies, out the door! It was like setting a stage. She ran about raising green shades to allow the summer in, flooding the rooms with bright color. The house was terribly lonely without a dog making noise like a typewriter on the kitchen floor or a cat blowing through it like silk tumbleweed over rose-patterned carpets, or the golden bird throbbing in its golden jail. The only sound now was the soft whisper that Grandma heard as her feverish body burned into old age.

In the center of the kitchen floor she dropped a pan of grease. "Well, look what I did!" she laughed. "Careful. Someone might slip and fall on that!" She did not mop it up, but sat on the far side of the kitchen.

"I'm ready," she announced to the silence.

The sunlight lay on her lap where she cradled a pot of peas. In her hand a paring knife moved to open them. Her fingers tumbled the green pods. Time passed. The kitchen was so quiet you heard the refrigerator humming behind its pressed-tight rubber seals around the door. Grandma smiled a pressed and similar smile and unhinged the pods.

The kitchen door opened and shut quietly.

"Oh!" Grandma dropped her pan.

"Hello, Grandma," said Tom.

On the floor, near the grease spot, the peas were strewn like a broken necklace.

"You're back," said Grandma.

"I'm back," Tom said. "Liddy's in Glendale. I left her to shop. Said I forgot something. Said I'd pick her up in an hour."

They looked at each other.

"I hear you're going East, Grandma," he said.

"That's funny, I heard *you* were," she said.

"All of a sudden you left without a word," he said.

"All of a sudden you packed up and went," she said.

"No, *you*," he said.

"You," she said.

He took a step toward the grease spot.

Water which had gathered in the sink was jarred by his moves. It trickled down the Garburator's throat, which gave off a gentle chuckling wet sound.

Tom did not look down as his shoe slipped on the grease.

"Tom." Sunlight flickered on Grandma's paring knife. "What can I *do* for you?"

The postman dropped six letters in the Barton mailbox and listened.

"There's that lion again," he said. "Here comes someone," said the postman. "Singing."

Footsteps neared the door. A voice sang:

"Fee fie foe fum,
I smell the blood of an Englishmun,
Be he alive or be he dead,
I'll grr-innnd *his bones to make my bread!"*

The door flew wide.
"Morning!" cried Grandma, smiling.
The lion roared.

Driving Blind

"**D**id you see that?"

"See what?"

"Why, hell, look *there!*"

But the big six-passenger 1929 Studebaker was already gone.

One of the men standing in front of Fremley's Hardware had stepped down off the curb to stare after the vehicle.

"That guy was driving with a hood over his head. Like a hangman's hood, black, over his head, driving blind!"

"I saw it, I saw it!" said a boy standing, similarly riven, nearby. The boy was me, Thomas Quincy Riley, better known as Tom or Quint and mighty curious. I ran. "Hey, wait up! Gosh! Driving *blind!*"

I almost caught up with the blind driver at Main and Elm where the Studebaker turned off down Elm followed by a siren. A town policeman on his motorcycle, stunned with the traveling vision, was giving pursuit.

When I reached the car it was double-parked with the officer's boot up on the running board and Willy Crenshaw, the officer, scowling in at the black Hood and someone under the Hood.

"Would you mind taking that thing off?" he said.

"No, but here's my driver's license," said a muffled voice. A hand with the license sailed out the window.

"I want to see your face," said Willy Crenshaw.

"It's right there on the license."

"I want to check and see if the two compare," said Willy Crenshaw.

"The name is Phil Dunlop," said the Hooded voice. "121 Desplaines Street, Gurney. Own the Studebaker Sales at 16 Gurney Avenue. It's all there if you can read."

Willy Crenshaw creased his forehead and inched his eyesight along the words.

"Hey, mister," I said. "This is real neat!"

"Shut up, son." The policeman ground his boot on the running board. "What you *up* to?"

I stood arching my feet, peering over the officer's shoulder as he hesitated to write up a ticket or jail a crook.

"What you *up* to?" Willy Crenshaw repeated.

"Right now," said the Hooded voice, "I'd like a place to stay overnight so I can prowl your town a few days."

Willy Crenshaw leaned forward. "What *kind* of prowling?"

"In this car, as you see, making people sit up and notice."

"They done that," the policeman admitted, looking at the crowd that had accumulated behind Thomas Quincy Riley, me.

"Is it a big crowd, boy?" said the man under the Hood.

I didn't realize he was addressing me, then I quickened up. "Sockdolager!" I said.

"You think if I drove around town twenty-four hours dressed like this, people might listen for one minute and hear what I *say?*"

"All ears," I said.

"There you have it, Officer," said the Hood, staring straight ahead, or what seemed like. "I'll stay on, 'cause the boy says. Boy," said the voice, "you know a good place for me to shave my unseen face and rest my feet?"

"My grandma, she—"

"Sounds good. Boy—"

"Name's Thomas Quincy Riley."

"Call you Quint?"

"How'd you guess?"

"Quint, jump in, show the way. But don't try to peek under my cover-up."

"No, *sir!*"

And I was around the car and in the front seat, my heart pure jackrabbit.

"Excuse us, Officer. Any questions, I'll be sequestered at this child's place."

"Six one nine Washington Street—" I began.

"I know, I know!" cried the officer. "Damnation."

"You'll let me go in this boy's custody?"

"Hell!" The policeman jerked his boot off the running board which let the car bang away.

"Quint?" said the voice under the dark Hood, steering. "What's *my* name?"

"You said—"

"No, no. What do *you* want to call me?"

"Hmm. Mr. Mysterious?"

"Bull's-eye. Where do I turn left, right, right, left, and right again?"

"Well," I said.

And we motored off, me terrified of collisions and Mr. Mysterious, real nice and calm, made a perfect left.

Some people knit because their fingers need preoccupations for their nerves.

Grandma didn't knit, but plucked peas from the pod. We had peas just about most nights in my life. Other nights she plucked lima beans. String beans? She harped on those, too, but they didn't pluck as easy or as neat as peas. Peas were it. As we came up the porch steps, Grandma eyed our arrival and shelled the little greens.

"Grandma," I said. "This is Mr. Mysterious."

"I could *see* that." Grandma nodded and smiled at she knew not what.

"He's wearing a Hood," I said.

"I noticed." Grandma was still unaffected and amiable.

"He needs a room."

"To need, the Bible says, is to have. Can he find his way up? Excuse the question."

"And *board*," I added.

"Beg pardon, how's he going to eat through that *thing*?"

"Hood," I said.

"Hood?"

"I can manage," Mr. Mysterious murmured.

"He can manage," I translated.

"That'll be worth watching." Grandma stitched out more green peas. "Sir, do you have a name?"

"I just *told* you," I said.

"So you did." Grandma nodded. "Dinner's at six," she said, "sharp."

The supper table, promptly at six, was loud with roomers and boarders. Grandpa having come home from Goldfield and Silver Creek, Nevada, with neither gold nor silver, and hiding out in the library parlor behind his books, allowed Grandma to room three bachelors and two bachelor ladies upstairs, while three boarders came in from various neighborhoods a few blocks away. It made for a lively breakfast, lunch, and dinner and Grandma made enough from this to keep our ark from sinking. Tonight there was five minutes of uproar concerning politics, three minutes on religion, and then the best talk about the food set before them, just as Mr. Mysterious arrived and everyone shut up. He glided among them, nodding his Hood right and left, and as he sat I yelled:

"Ladies and gentlemen, meet Mr.—"

"Just call me Phil," murmured Mr. Mysterious.

I sat back, somewhat aggrieved.

"Phil," said everyone.

They all stared at him and couldn't tell if he saw their stares through the black velvet. How's he going to eat, hid like that, they thought. Mr. Mysterious picked up a big soup spoon.

"Pass the gravy, please," he whispered.

"Pass the mashed potatoes," he added quietly.

"Pass the peas," he finished.

"Also, Mrs. Grandma . . ." he said. Grandma, in the doorway, smiled. It seemed a nice touch: "Mrs." He said, ". . . please bring me my blue-plate special."

Grandma placed what was indeed a Chinese garden done in blue ceramics but containing what looked to be a dog's dinner. Mr. Mysterious ladled the gravy, the mashed potatoes, and the peas on and mashed and crushed it shapeless as we watched, trying not to bug our eyes.

There was a moment of silence as the voice under the dark Hood said, "Anyone mind if I say grace?"

Nobody would mind.

"O Lord," said the hidden voice, "let us receive those gifts of love that shape and change and move our lives to perfection. May others see in us only what we see in them, perfection and beauty beyond telling. Amen."

"Amen," said all as Mr. M. snuck from his coat a thing to astonish the boarders and amaze the rest.

"That," someone said (me), "is the biggest darn soda fountain straw I ever seen!"

"Quint!" said Grandma.

"Well, it *is!*"

And it was. A soda fountain straw two or three times larger than ordinary which vanished up under the Hood and probed down through the mashed potatoes, peas, and gravy dog's dinner which silently ascended the straw to vanish in an unseen mouth, silent and soundless as cats at mealtime.

Which made the rest of us fall to, self-consciously cutting, chewing, and swallowing so loud we all blushed.

While Mr. Mysterious sucked his liquid victuals up out of sight with not even so much as a purr. From the corners of our eyes we watched the victuals slide silently and invisibly under the Hood until the plate was hound's-tooth clean. And all this done with Mr. M.'s fingers and hands fixed to his knees.

"I—" said Grandma, her gaze on that straw, "hope you liked your dinner, sir."

"Sockdolager," said Mr. Mysterious.

"Ice cream's for dessert," said Grandma. "Mostly melted."

"Melted!" Mr. M. laughed.

*   *   *

It was a fine summer night with three cigars, one cigarette, and assorted knitting on the front porch and enough rocking chairs going somewhere-in-place to make dogs nervous and cats leave.

In the clouds of cigar smoke and a pause in the knitting, Grandpa, who always came out after dark, said:

"If you don't mind my infernal nerve, now that you're settled in, what's *next?*"

Mr. Mysterious, leaning on the front porch rail, looking, we supposed, out at his shiny Studebaker, put a cigarette to his Hood and drew some smoke in, then out without coughing. I stood watching, proudly.

"Well," said Mr. M., "I got several roads to take. See that car out there?"

"It's large and obvious," said Grandpa.

"That is a brand-new class-A Studebaker Eight, got thirty miles on it, which is as far from Gurney to here and a few runaround blocks. My car salesroom is just about big enough to hold three Studebakers and four customers at once. Mostly dairy farmers pass my windows but don't come in. I figured it was time to come to a live-wire place, where if I shouted 'Leap' you might at least hop."

"We're waiting," said Grandpa.

"Would you like a small demonstration of what I pray for and *will* realize?" said the cigarette smoke wafting out through the fabric in syllables. "Someone say 'Go.'"

Lots of cigar smoke came out in an explosion.

"Go!"

"Jump, Quint!"

I reached the Studebaker before him and Mr. Mysterious was no sooner in the front seat than we took off.

"Right and then left and then right, correct, Quint?"

And right, left, right it was to Main Street and us banging away fast.

"Don't laugh so loud, Quint."

"Can't help it! This is *peacherino!*"

"Stop swearing. Anyone following?"

"Three young guys on the sidewalk here. Three old gents off the curb there!"

He slowed. The six following us soon became eight.

"Are we almost at the cigar-store corner where the loudmouths hang out, Quint?"

"You *know* we are."

"Watch this!"

As we passed the cigar store he slowed and choked the gas. The most terrific Fourth of July BANG fired out the exhaust. The cigar-store loudmouths jumped a foot and grabbed their straw hats. Mr. M. gave them another BANG, accelerated, and the eight following soon was a dozen.

"Hot diggity!" cried Mr. Mysterious. "Feel their love, Quint? Feel their *need?* Nothing like a brand-new eight-cylinder super prime A-1 Studebaker to make a man feel like Helen just passed through Troy! I'll stop now that there's folks enough for arguments to possess and fights to keep. *So!*"

We stopped dead-center on Main and Arbogast as the moths collected to our flame.

"Is that a brand-new just-out-of-the-showroom Studebaker?" said our town barber. The fuzz behind my ears knew him well.

"Absolutely spanking brand-new," said Mr. M.

"*I* was here first, *I* get to ask!" cried the mayor's assistant, Mr. Bagadosian.

"Yeah, but *I* got the money!" A third man stepped into the dashboard light. Mr. Bengstrom, the man who owned the graveyard and everyone *in* it.

"Got only *one* Studebaker now," said the sheepish voice under the Hood. "Wish I had more."

That set off a frenzy of remorse and tumult.

"The entire price," said Mr. M. in the midst of the turmoil, "is eight hundred and fifty dollars. The first among you who slaps a fifty-dollar bill or its equivalent in singles, fives, and tens in my hand gets to pink-slip this mythological warship home."

No sooner was Mr. Mysterious' palm out the window than it was plastered with fives, tens, and twenties.

"Quint?"

"Sir?"

"Reach in that cubby and drag out my order forms."

"Yes, *sir!*"

"Bengstrom! Cyril A. Bengstrom!" the undertaker cried so he could be heard.

"Be calm, Mr. Bengstrom. The car is yours. Sign *here.*"

Moments later, Mr. Bengstrom, laughing hysterically, drove off from a sullen mob at Main and Arbogast. He circled us twice to make the abandoned crowd even more depressed then roared off to find a highway and test his craze.

"Don't fret," said the voice under the dark Hood. "I got one last Studebaker prime A-1 vehicle, or maybe two, waiting back in Gurney. Someone drop me there?"

"Me!" said everyone.

"So *that's* the way you function," said Grandpa. *"That's* why you're here."

It was later in the evening with more mosquitoes and fewer knitters and smokers. Another Studebaker, bright red, stood out at the curb. "Wait till they see the sun shine on *this* one," said Mr. Mysterious, laughing gently.

"I have a feeling you'll sell your entire line this week," said Grandpa, "and leave us wanting."

"I'd rather not talk futures and sound uppity, but so it seems."

"Sly fox." Grandpa tamped philosophy in his pipe and puffed it out. "Wearing that sack over your head to focus need and provoke talk."

"It's more than that." Mr. M. sucked, tucking a cigarette through the dark material over his mouth. "More than a trick. More than a come-on. More than a passing fancy."

"What?" said Grandpa.

*   *   *

"What?" I said.

It was midnight and I couldn't sleep.

Neither could Mr. Mysterious. I crept downstairs and found him in the backyard in a wooden summer recliner perhaps studying the fireflies and beyond them the stars, some holding still, others not.

"Hello, Quint!" he said.

"Mr. Mysterious?" I said.

"*Ask* me."

"You wear that Hood even when you *sleep?*"

"All night long every night."

"For most of your life?"

"Almost most."

"Last night you said it's more than a trick, showing off. What *else?*"

"If I didn't tell the roomers and your grandpa, why should I tell you, Quint?" said the Hood with no features resting there in the night.

" 'Cause I want to know."

"That's about the best reason in the world. Sit down, Quint. Aren't the fireflies nice?"

I sat on the wet grass. "Yeah."

"Okay," said Mr. Mysterious, and turned his head under his Hood as if he were staring at me. "Here goes. Ever wonder what's under this Hood, Quint? Ever have the itch to yank it off and see?"

"Nope."

"Why not?"

"That lady in *The Phantom of the Opera* did. Look where it got *her*."

"Then shall I *tell* you what's hidden, son?"

"Only if you want to, sir."

"Funny thing is, I do. This Hood goes back a long way."

"From when you were a kid?"

"Almost. I can't recall if I was born this way or something happened. Car accident. Fire. Or some woman laughing at me which burned just as bad, scarred just as terrible. One way or another we fall off buildings or fall out of bed. When we hit the floor it might as well have been off the roof. It takes a long time healing. Maybe never."

"You mean you don't remember when you put that thing on?"

"Things fade, Quint. I have lived in confusion a long while. This dark stuff has been such a part of me it might just be my living flesh."

"Do—"

"Do what, Quint?"

"Do you sometimes *shave?*"

"No, it's all smooth. You can imagine me two ways, I suppose. It's all nightmare under here, all graveyards, terrible teeth, skulls and wounds that won't heal. Or—"

"Or?"

"Nothing at all. Absolutely nothing. No beard for shaving. No eyebrows. Mostly no nose. Hardly any eyelids, just eyes. Hardly any mouth; a scar. The rest a vacancy, a snowfield, a blank, as if someone had erased

91

me to start over. There. Two ways of guessing. Which do you pick?"

"I can't."

"No."

Mr. Mysterious arose now and stood barefooted on the grass, his Hood pointed at some star constellation.

"You," I said, at last. "You still haven't told what you started tonight to tell Grandpa. You came here not just to sell brand-new Studebakers—but for something else?"

"Ah." He nodded. "Well. I been alone a lot of years. It's no fun over in Gurney, just selling cars and hiding under this velvet sack. So I decided to come out in the open at last and mix with honest-to-goodness people, make friends, maybe get someone to like me or at least put up with me. You understand, Quint?"

"I'm trying."

"What good will all this do, living in Green Town and thriving at your supper table and viewing the tree-tops in my cupola tower room? *Ask.*"

"What good?" I asked.

"What I'm hoping for, Quint, what I'm praying for, son, is that if I delve in the river again, wade in the stream, become part of the flow of folks, people, strangers even, some sort of kind attention, friendship, some sort of half-love will begin to melt and change my face. Over six or eight months or a year, to let life shift my mask without lifting it, so that the wax beneath moves and becomes something more than a nightmare at three a.m. or just nothing at dawn. Any of this make sense, Quint?"

"Yeah. I guess."

"For people *do* change us, don't they? I mean you run in and out of this house and your grandpa changes you and your grandpa shapes you with words or a hug or your hair tousled or maybe once a year, a slap where it hurts."

"Twice."

"Twice, then. And the boarders and roomers talk and you listen and that goes in your ears and out your fingers and that's change, too. We're all in the wash, all in the creeks, all in the streams, taking in every morsel of gab, every push from a teacher, every shove from a bully, every look and touch from those strange creatures, for *you* called women. Sustenance. It's all breakfast tea and midnight snacks and you grow on it or you don't grow, laugh or scowl or don't have any features one way or the other, but *you're* out there, melting and freezing, running or holding still. I haven't done that in years. So just this week I got up my courage—knew how to sell cars but didn't know how to put *me* on sale. I'm taking a chance, Quint, that by next year, this face under the Hood will make itself over, shift at noon or twilight, and I'll feel it changing because I'm out wading in the stream again and breathing the fresh air and letting people get at me, taking a chance, not hiding behind the windshield of this or that Studebaker. And at the end of that next year, Quint, I'll take off my Hood forever."

At which point, turned away from me, he made a gesture. I saw the dark velvet in his hand as he dropped it in the grass.

"Do you want to see what's here, Quint?" he asked, quietly.

"No, sir, if you don't mind."

"Why not?"

"I'm scared," I said, and shivered.

"That figures," he said, at last. "I'll just stand here a moment and then hide again."

He took three deep breaths, his back to me, head high, face toward the fireflies and a few constellations. Then the Hood was back in place.

I'm glad, I thought, there's no moon tonight.

Five days and five Studebakers later (one blue, one black, two tans, and one sunset-red) Mr. Mysterious was sitting out in what he said was his final car, a sun-yellow open roadster, so bright it was a canary with its own cage, when I came strolling out, hands in overall pockets, watching the sidewalk for ants or old unused firecrackers. When Mr. M. saw me he moved over and said, "Try the driver's seat."

"Boy! *Can* I?"

I did, and twirled the wheel and honked the horn, just once, so as not to wake any late-sleepers.

" 'Fess up, Quint," said Mr. Mysterious, his Hood pointed out through the windshield.

"Do I look like I need 'fessing'?"

"You're ripe-plumful. Begin."

"I been thinking," I said.

"I could tell by the wrinkles in your face," said Mr. M., gently.

"I been thinking about a year from now, and you."

"That's mighty nice, son. Continue."

"I thought, well, maybe next year if you felt you were cured, under that Hood, that your nose was okay and your eyebrows neat, and your mouth good and your complexion—"

I hesitated. The Hood nodded me on.

"Well, I was thinking if you got up one morning and without even putting your hands up to feel underneath you knew the long waiting was over and you were changed, people and things had changed you, the town, everything, and you were great, just great, no way of *ever* going back to nothing."

"Go on, Quint."

"Well, if that happened, Mr. Mysterious, and you just *knew* you were really great to see forever, why then, Mr. M., you wouldn't *have* to take off your Hood, *would* you?"

"What'd you *say*, son?"

"I said, you wouldn't have to ta—"

"I heard you, Quint, I heard," gasped Mr. M.

There was a long silence. He made some strange sounds, almost like choking, and then he whispered hoarsely, "No, I wouldn't need to take off my Hood."

" 'Cause it wouldn't matter, would it? If you really knew that underneath, everything was okay. Sure?"

95

"Oh, Lord yes, sure."

"And you could wear the Hood for the next hundred years and only you and me would know what's underneath. And we wouldn't tell or care."

"Just you and me. And what would I look like under the Hood, Quint? Sockdolager?"

"Yes, sir."

There was a long silence and Mr. Mysterious' shoulders shook a few times and he made a quiet choking sound and all of a sudden some water dripped off the bottom of his Hood.

I stared at it. "Oh," I said.

"It's all right, Quint," he said, quietly. "It's just tears."

"Gosh."

"It's all right. Happy tears."

Mr. Mysterious got out of the last Studebaker then and touched at his invisible nose and dabbed at the cloth in front of his unseen eyes.

"Quintessential Quint," he said. "No one else like you in the whole world."

"Heck, that goes for *everyone*, don't it?"

"If you say so, Quint."

Then he added:

"Got any last things to upchuck or confess, son?"

"Some silly stuff. What if—?"

I paused and swallowed and could only look ahead through the steering wheel spokes at the naked silver lady on the hood.

"What if, a long time ago, you never *needed* the Hood?"

"You mean never? Never *ever?*"

"Yes, sir. What if a long time ago you only *thought* you needed to hide and put on that stuff with no eye-holes even. What if there was never any accident, or fire, or you weren't born that way, or no lady ever laughed at you, what *then?*"

"You mean I only imagined I had to put on this sackcloth and ashes? And all these years I been walking around thinking there *was* something awful or just nothing, a blank underneath?"

"It just came to me."

There was a long silence.

"And all these years I been walking around not knowing or pretending I had something to hide, for no reason, because my face was there all the time, mouth, cheeks, eyebrows, nose, and didn't need melting down to be fixed?"

"I didn't mean—"

"You *did.*" A final tear fell off the bottom rim of his Hood. "How old are you, Quint?"

"Going on thirteen."

"No. Methuselah."

"He was *real* old. But did he have any jellybeans in his *head?*"

"Like you, Quincy. A marvel of jellybeans."

There was a long silence, then he said:

"Walk around town? Need to flex my legs. Walk?"

We turned right at Central, left at Grand, right again

at Genesee, and stopped in front of the Karcher Hotel, twelve stories, the highest building in Green County or beyond.

"Quint?"

His Hood pointed up along the building while his voice under observed. "Thomas Quincy Riley, you got that *one last thing* look. Spit it out."

I hesitated and said, "Well. Up inside that Hood, is it *really* dark? I mean, there's no radio gadgets or see-back-oscopes or secret holes?"

"Thomas Quincy Riley, you been reading the Johnson Smith & Co. Tricks, Toys, Games and Halloween Catalogue from Racine, Wisconsin."

"Can't help it."

"Well, when I die you'll inherit this sack, wear it, and know darkness."

The head turned and I could almost feel his eyes burn the dark material.

"Right now, I can look through your ribs and see your heart like a flower or a fist, opening, closing, open, shut. You believe that?"

I put my fist on my chest.

"Yes, sir," I said.

"Now."

He turned to point his Hood up along the hotel for twelve stories.

"Know what I been thinking?"

"Sir?"

"Stop calling myself Mr. Mysterious."

"Oh, *no!*"

"Hold on! I've done what I came for. Car sales are runaway. Hallelujah. But look, Quint. Look up and touch. What if I became the Human Fly?"

I gasped. "You mean—"

"Yessireebob. Can't you just see me up six stories and eight and twelve at the top, with my Hood still on, waving down at the crowd?"

"Gee!"

"Glad for your approval." Mr. M. stepped forward and started to climb, reaching for holds, finding, and climbing more. When he was three feet up he said, "What's a good *tall* name for a Human Fly?"

I shut my eyes, then said:

"*High*tower!"

"Hightower, by God! Do we go home to breakfast?"

"Yes, *sir*."

"Mashed bananas, mashed cornflakes, mashed oatmeal—"

"Ice cream!" I added.

"Melted," said the Human Fly and climbed back down.

I Wonder What's Become of Sally

Somebody started playing the yellow-keyed piano, somebody started singing, and somebody, myself, started thinking. The words of the song were slow, sweet, and sad:

> *"I wonder what's become of Sally,*
> *That old gal of mine."*

I hummed it. I remembered some more words:

> *"The sunshine's gone from out our alley,*
> *Ever since the day Sally went away."*

"I knew a Sally once," I said.
"You did?" said the bartender, not looking at me.
"Sure," I said. "Very first girlfriend. Like the words

of that song, makes you wonder, whatever happened to her? Where's she tonight? About all you can do is hope she's happy, married, got five kids, and a husband who isn't late more than once a week, and remembers, or doesn't remember, her birthdays, whichever way she likes it most."

"Why don't you look her up?" said the bartender, still not looking at me, shining a glass.

I drank my drink slowly.

> *"Wherever she may go,*
> *Wherever she may be,*
> *If no one wants her now,*
> *Please send her back to me."*

The people around the piano were finishing the song. I listened, eyes shut.

> *"I wonder what's become of Sally,*
> *That old gal of mine."*

The piano stopped. There was a lot of quiet laughter and talk.

I put the empty glass down on the bar and opened my eyes and looked at it for a minute.

"You know," I said to the bartender, "you just gave me an idea . . ."

Where do I start? I thought, outside on the rainy street in a cold wind, night coming on, buses and cars moving by, the world suddenly alive with sound. Or do you start at all, which is it?

I'd had ideas like this before; I got them all the time. On Sunday afternoons if I overslept I woke up thinking I had heard someone crying and found tears on my face and wondered what year it was and sometimes had to go off and find a calendar just to be sure. On those Sundays I felt there was fog outside the house, and had to go open the door to be sure the sun was still slanting across the lawn. It wasn't anything I could control. It just happened while I was half asleep and the old years gathered around and the light changed. Once, on a Sunday like that, I telephoned clear across the United States to an old school chum, Bob Hartmann. He was glad to hear my voice, or said he was, and we talked for half an hour and it was a nice talk, full of promises. But we never got together, as we had planned; next year, when he came to town, I was in a different mood. But that's how those things go, isn't it? Warm and mellow one second, and the next I looked around and I was gone.

But right now, standing on the street outside of Mike's Bar, I held out my hand and added up my fingers: first, my wife was out of town visiting her mother downstate. Second, tonight was Friday, and a whole free weekend ahead. Third, I remembered Sally very well, if no one else did. Fourth, I just wanted somehow to say, Hello, Sally, how are things? Fifth, why didn't I start?

I did.

*   *   *

I got the phone book and went down the lists. Sally Ames. Ames, Ames. I looked at them all. Of course. She was married. That was the bad thing about women: once married they took aliases, vanishing into the earth, and you were lost.

Well then, her parents, I thought.

They were unlisted. Moved or dead.

What about some of her old friends who were once friends of mine? Joan something-or-other. Bob whatsisname. I drew blanks, and then remembered someone named Tom Welles.

I found Tom in the book and telephoned him.

"Good God, is that you, Charlie?" he cried. "Good grief, come on over. What's new? Lord, it's been years! Why are you—"

I told him what I was calling about.

"Sally? Haven't seen her in years. Hey, I hear you're doing okay, Charlie. Salary in five figures, right? Pretty good for a guy from across the tracks."

There hadn't been any tracks, really; just an invisible line nobody could see but everyone felt.

"Hey, when can we see you, Charlie?"

"Give you a call soon."

"She was a sweet girl, Sally. I've told my wife about her. Those eyes. And hair color that didn't come out of a bottle. And—"

As Tom talked on, a lot of things came back. The way she listened, or pretended to listen, to all my grand talk about the future. It suddenly seemed she had never talked at all. I wouldn't let her. With the sublime dumb ego of a young man I filled up the nights and days with building tomorrows and tearing them down and building them again, just for her. Looking back, I was embarrassed for myself. And then I remembered how her eyes used to take fire and her cheeks flush with my talking, as if everything I said was worth her time and life and blood. But in all the talk, I couldn't remember ever saying I loved her. I should have. I never touched her, save to hold her hand, and never kissed her. That was a sadness now. But I had been afraid that if I ever made one mistake, like kissing, she would dissolve like snow on a summer night, and be gone forever. We went together and talked together, or I talked, rather, for a year. I couldn't remember why we broke up. Suddenly, for no reason, she was gone, around the same time we both left school forever. I shook my head, eyes shut.

"Do you remember, she wanted to be a singer once, she had a swell voice," said Tom. "She—"

"Sure," I said. "It all comes back. So long."

"Wait a minute—" said his voice, being hung back on the receiver hook.

I went back to the old neighborhood and walked around. I went in the grocery stores and asked. I saw a few people who I knew but who didn't remember me. And finally I got a line on her. Yes, she was married. No, they weren't sure of the address. Yes, *his* name was Maretti. Somewhere on that street down that way and over a few blocks, or maybe it was the other way.

I checked the name I the phone book. That should have warned me. No phone.

Then by asking questions at some grocery stores down the line, I finally got the Maretti address. Third apartment, fourth floor, rear, number 407.

"Why are you doing this?" I asked myself, going up the stairs, climbing in the dim light in the smell of old food and dust. "Want to show her how well you've done, is *that* it?

"No," I told myself. "I just want to see Sally, someone from the old days. I want to get around to telling her what I should have told her years ago, that, in my own way, at one time, I loved her. I never told her that. But I was afraid. I'm not afraid now that it doesn't make any difference.

"You're a fool," I said.

"Yes," I said, "but aren't we all."

I had to stop to rest on the third landing. I had a feeling, suddenly, in the thick smell of ancient cooking, in the close, whispering darkness of TVs playing too loud and distant children crying, that I should walk down out of the house before it was too late.

"But you've come this far. Come on," I said. "One more flight."

I went up the last stairs slowly and stood before an unpainted door. Behind it, people moved and children talked. I hesitated. What would I say? Hello, Sally, remember the old days when we went boating in the park and the trees were green and you were as slender as a blade of grass? Remember the time that—well.

I raised my hand.

I knocked on the door.

It opened and a woman answered. I'd say she was about ten years older, maybe fifteen, than me. She was wearing a two-dollar basement dress which didn't fit, and her hair was turning gray. There was a lot of fat in the wrong places, and lines around her tired mouth. I almost said, "I've got the wrong apartment, I'm looking for Sally Maretti." But I didn't say anything. Sally was a good five years younger than me. But this was she, looking out of the door into the dim light. Behind her was a room with a battered lampshade, a linoleum floor, one table, and some old brown overstuffed furniture.

We stood looking at each other across twenty-five years. What could I say? Hello, Sally, I'm back, here I am, prosperous, on the other side of town now, here I am, a good car, home, married, children through school, here I am president of a company, why didn't you marry me and you wouldn't be here? I saw her eyes move to my Masonic ring, to the boutonniere in my lapel, to the clean rim of the new hat in my hand, to my gloves, to my shined shoes, to my Florida-tanned face, to my Bronzini tie. Then her eyes came back to my face. She was waiting for me to do one thing or the other. I did the right thing.

"I beg your pardon," I said. "I'm selling insurance."

"I'm sorry," she said. "We don't need any."

She held the door open for just a moment as if at any moment she might burst open.

"Sorry to have bothered you," I said.

"That's all right," she said.

I looked beyond her shoulder. I had been wrong. There were not five children, but six at the dinner table with the husband, a dark man with a scowl stamped on his brow.

"Close the door!" he said. "There's a draft."

"Good night," I said.

"Good night," she said.

I stepped back and she closed the door, her eyes still on my face.

I turned and went down the street.

I had just stepped off the bottom of the brownstone steps when I heard a voice call out behind me. It was a woman's voice. I kept walking. The voice called again and I slowed, but did not turn. A moment later someone put a hand on my elbow. Only then did I stop and look around.

It was the woman from apartment 407 above, her eyes almost wild, her mouth gasping, on the point of tears.

"I'm sorry," she said, and almost pulled back but then gathered herself to say, "This is crazy. You don't happen to be, I know you're not, you aren't Charlie McGraw, *are* you?"

I hesitated while her eyes searched my face, looking for some halfway familiar feature among all the oldness.

My silence made her uneasy. "No, I didn't really think you were," she said.

"I'm sorry," I said. "Who was he?"

"Oh, God," she said, eyes down, stifling something like a laugh. "I don't know. Maybe a boyfriend, a long time ago."

I took her hand and held it for a moment. "I wish I were," I said. "We should have had a lot to talk about."

"Too much, maybe." A single tear fell from her cheek. She backed off. "Well, you can't have everything."

"No," I said, and gave her back her hand, gently.

My gentleness provoked her to a last question.

"You're *sure* you're not Charlie?"

"Charlie must've been a nice fellow."

"The best," she said.

"Well," I said, at last. "So long."

"No," she said. "Good-bye." She spun about and ran to the steps and ran up the steps so quickly that she almost tripped. At the top she whirled suddenly, her eyes brimmed, and lifted her hand to wave. I tried not to wave back but my hand went up.

I stood rooted to the sidewalk for a full half minute before I could make myself move. Jesus, I thought, every love affair I ever had I ruined.

I got back to the bar near closing time. The pianist, for some obscure reason, hating to go home was probably it, was still there.

Taking a double shot of brandy and working on a beer, I said,

"Whatever you do, don't play that piece about

wherever she may go, wherever she may be, if no one wants her now, please send her back to me . . ."

"What song is that?" said the pianist, hands on the keys.

"Something," I said. "Something about . . . what was her name? Oh, yeah. Sally."

Nothing Changes

There is this truly wonderful bookstore by the ocean where you can hear the tide under the pier, shaking the shop, the books on the shelves, and you.

The shop is dark and has a tin roof above the ten thousand books from which you blow dust in order to turn pages.

And it is not just the tide below but the tide above that I love when storm rains shatter that tin roof, banging it like orchestras of machine-gun-cymbal-and-drum. Whenever it is a dark midnight at noon, if not in my soul, like Ishmael, I head for the storm beneath and the storm above, tambourining the tin and knocking silverfish off forgotten authors, row on row. With my smile for a flashlight, I linger all day.

Pure hyperventilation in storms, I arrived one noon at White Whale Books, where I walked, slowly, to the entrance. My anxious taxi driver pursued with his umbrella. I held him off. "Please," I said. "I *want* to get wet!"

"Nut!" cried the cabbie and left.

Gloriously damp, I ducked inside, shook myself like a dog, and froze, eyes shut, hearing the rain bang that high tin roof.

"Which way?" I said to the darkness.

Intuition said left.

I turned and found, in the tintinnabulation of downpour (what a great word: tintinnabulation!) stacks of shelves of old high school annuals which I usually avoid like funerals.

For bookshops are, by their nature, graveyards where old elephants drop their bones.

Uneasily, then, I prowled the high school yearbooks to read the spines: Burlington, Vermont, Orange, New Jersey, Roswell, New Mexico, big sandwiches of memorabilia from fifty states. I did not touch my own godforsaken yearbook, which lay buried with its scribbled time-capsule insults from the Great Depression: "Get lost, sappo. Jim." "Have a great life, you should live so long. Sam." "To a fine writer, lousy lover. Fay."

I blew the dust off Remington High, Pennsylvania, to thumb through scores of baseball, basketball, football braves no longer brave.

1912.

I scanned ten dozen bright faces.

You, you, and you, I thought. Was your life good? Did you marry well? Did your kids like you? Was there a great first love and another later? How, how did it *go?*

Too many flowers here from too many biers. All those eager eyes staring above their wondrous smiles.

I almost shut the book but . . .

My finger stayed on the pictures of the 1912 graduating class, with World War I not yet, unimagined and unknown, when I blinked at one snapshot and gasped:

"My God! Charles! Old Charlie *Nesbitt!*"

Yes! Framed there in a far year, with his freckles, roostercomb hair, big ears, flared nostrils, and corncob teeth. Charles Woodley Nesbitt!

"Charlie!" I cried.

The rain buckshot the tin roof above. The cold blew down my neck.

"Charlie," I whispered. "What're you doing *here?*"

I carried the book out to a better light, heart thumping, and stared.

The name under the picture was Reynolds. Winton Reynolds.

Destined for Harvard
Wants to make a million.
Likes golf.

But the *picture?*
"*Charlie*, dammit!"

Charlie Nesbitt was god-awful homely, a tennis pro, top gymnast, speed swimmer, girl collector. How come? Did those ears, teeth, and nostrils make girls swarm? To *be* like him, we would have signed up for lessons.

And now here he was on a wrong page of an old

book in a lost year with his berserk smile and crazed ears.

Could there once have been *two* Charlie Nesbitts alive? Identical twins, separated at birth? Hell. *My* Charlie was born in 1920, same as me. Wait!

I dodged back in the stacks to grab my 1938 yearbook and riffle the graduate photos until I found:

Wants to be a golf pro.
Heads for Princeton.
Hopes to be rich.

Charles Woodley Nesbitt.

The same goofy teeth, ears, and multitudinous freckles!

I placed the two annuals to study these seeming "twins."

Seemed? No! *Absolutely* the *same!*

Rain drummed the high tin roof.

"Hell, Charlie, hell, Winton!"

I carried the books up front where Mr. Lemley, as old as his books, peered at me over his Ben Franklin specs.

"Found *those*, did you? Take 'em. Free."

"Mr. Lemley, look . . ."

I showed him the pictures and the names.

"I'll be damned." He snorted. "Same family? Brothers? Naw. Same fella, though. How'd you find this?"

"Just did."

"Give me the collywobbles. Coincidence. One in a million births, right?"

"Yeah." I turned the pages back and forth, over and over. "But what if all the faces in *all* the annuals in all the towns in all the states, hell, what if they *all look* alike!

"What'd I just *say?*" I cried, hearing myself.

What if *all* the faces in all the annuals were the *same!*

"Outta the way!" I shouted.

Tearing up the cabbage patch is how Mr. Lemley told it later. If the God of Vengeance and Terror was Shiva with many arms, I was a small but louder god, with a dozen hands seizing books, cursing at revelations, frights, and elations, alone, as witness to a big parade marching nowhere, with separate bands and different choirs in towns strewn across a blind world. From time to time as I leaped through the stacks, Mr. Lemley brought coffee and whispered: "Rest up."

"You don't understand!" I cried.

"No, I don't. How *old* are you?"

"Forty-nine!"

"Act like a nine-year-old running up the aisle at a bad movie, peeing."

"Good advice!" I ran and came back.

Mr. Lemley checked the linoleum for wet spots. "Continue."

I seized more annuals:

"Ella, there's Ella *again*. Tom, there's Tom who looks like Joe, and Frank, a dead ringer for Ralph. Ringer, hell, spittin' *image!* And Helen who's a twin to Cora!

And Ed and Phil and Morris to fit Roger and Alan and Pat. Christ!"

I had two dozen books butterflied, some torn in my haste. "I'll pay, Mr. Lemley, I'll *pay!*"

In the mist of the storm-fever I stopped on page 47 of the Cheyenne 1911 *Book of High School Remembrances*.

For there was the sap, the simpleton, the ignoramus, the shy wimp, the lost soul.

His name, in that lost year?

DOUGLAS DRISCOLL.

His message to the future?

Admired as a thespian.
Will soon join the unemployed.
Headed for literary distinction.

Poor fool, lost dreamer, final achiever.

Douglas Driscoll, Cheyenne, 1911.

Me.

My eyes streaming tears, I bumped my way out of the twilight stacks to show my melancholy gift to Mr. Lemley.

"Gosh." He touched the picture. "That *can't* be someone named Driscoll.

"That's got to be," he said, *"you."*

"Yes, sir."

"Damn," he said, softly. "You *know* this boy?"

"No."

"Got any relatives in . . . Wyoming?"

"No, sir."

"How'd you come on this?"

"Wild hunch."

"Yeah, you really tore up the tundra." He studied my identical twin, half a century ago. "What will you do? Look this fella *up*?"

"If graveyards count for looking."

"It *is* a long time back. How about his kids, or *grand*kids?"

"What would I tell them? They wouldn't necessarily look like him anyway."

"Hell," said Mr. Lemley. "If one kid looks like you, 1911, why not someone *close*. Twenty years ago, or, hot damn, *this* year?"

"Repeat that!" I cried.

"*This* year?"

"You *got* some? *This* year's yearbooks?"

"God, I dunno. Hey, why are you *doing* this?"

"You ever feel," I shouted, "you're on the verge of a bombshell annihilating discovery?"

"Swimming once I found a big chunk of something awful. Ambergris! I thought. Sell it to a perfume factory for thousands! I ran to show the damned stuff to the lifeguard. Ambergris? Horseflies! I flung it back in the sea. *That* kind of annihilating discovery?"

"Maybe. Genealogies. Genetics."

"From what year?"

"Lincoln," I said. "Washington, Henry the Eighth. God, I feel as if I found all Creation, some obvious truth that's been sitting right in front of us forever and we didn't see. This could change history!"

"Or spoil it," said Mr. Lemley. "You sure you ain't been drinking back there in the stacks? Don't stand there. Go!"

"One side or a leg-off," I said.

I read and tossed, tossed and read, but there were no really new annuals. Phone calls and airmail was the answer.

"Jeez Christopher," observed Mr. Lemley. "Can you afford to *do* that?"

"I'll die if I don't."

"And die if you do. Closing time. Lights out."

The annuals streamed in during the week before graduations all across the country.

I stayed up two nights, sleepless, riffling, Xeroxing pages, tallying lists, twinning pasteups of ten dozen new faces against ten dozen old.

Christ, I thought, you damn stupid blind idiot on a runaway train. How do you steer? Where the hell is it going? And, oh God, *why?*

I had no answers. Gone mad, I mailed and phoned, sent and got back, like a blind man in a closet sorting clothes, trying inanities, discarding reason.

The mail was an avalanche.

It could not be, and yet it was. All biological rules? Out the window. The history of flesh was what? Darwinian "Sport." Genetic accidents that birthed new species. Derailed genes which spun the world afresh. But what if there were freak/sport replays? What if Nature hiccuped, and its needle jumped *back?* Then, having lost its genetic mind, wouldn't it clone generation after generation of Williamses, Browns, and Smiths? Not related by family, no. But mindless rebirths, blind matter trapped in a mirror maze? Impossible.

Yet there it was. Dozens of faces repeated in hundreds of faces across the world! Twin upon twin, *in excelsis*. And where did that leave room for new flesh, a history of progress and survival?

Shut up, I thought, and drink your gin.

The cascade of high school annuals continued.

I flipped their pages like decks of cards until, at last . . .

There it was.

Its arrival blew a hole in my stomach.

There was a name on page 124 of the Roswell High annual, published this week and just arrived. The name was:

William Clark Henderson.

I stared at his picture and saw:

Me.

Alive and graduating this week!

The other me.

An exact replica of every eyelash, eyebrow, small pore and large, ear fuzz and nostril hair.

Me. Myself. I.

No! I thought. I looked again. *Yes!*

I jumped. I ran.

Lugging a folder of pictures, I flew to Roswell and, sweating, grabbed a cab to reach Roswell High at twelve noon straight up.

The graduation procession had begun. I panicked. But then as the young men and women passed an immense calmness touched me. Destiny and Providence whispered as my gaze wandered over two hundred young faces in line and at some late-arriving wild smiles, manic with joy now that the long haul was over.

And still the young moved on their way to good or unborn wars, bad marriages, fine or awful employments.

And there *he* was. William Clark Henderson.

The other me.

As he walked, laughing, with a pretty dark-haired girl, I traced my own profile in my high school annual long ago. I saw the soft line under his chin, the unshaven cheeks, the unfocused half-blind eyes that would never understand life but hide out in libraries, duck behind typewriters.

As he passed, he glanced up and froze.

I almost waved, but stopped for he could not make himself move.

He staggered as if struck in the chest. His face grew pale as he groped toward me and gasped.

"Dad! What're you doing *here?*"

I felt my heart stop.

"You *can't* be here!" the young man cried, tears brimming his eyes. "You're *dead!* Died two years ago! Can't be. What? How?"

"No." I said at last. "I'm not . . ."

"Dad!" He seized my arms. "Oh, God! God!"

"Don't!" I said. "Not me!"

"Then *who?*" he pleaded and crushed his head against my chest. "What's going *on?* Christ!"

"Please." I broke his grip. "They're *waiting!*"

He fell back. "I don't understand," he said, the tears flowing.

"*I* don't understand," I said.

He lurched forward. I raised my hand swiftly. "No. Don't."

"Will you," he mourned, "be here . . . *after?*"

"Yes," I said, agonized. "No. I don't *know.*"

"At least *watch*," he said.

I was silent.

"Please," he said.

At last I nodded and saw color in his face.

"What's going *on?*" he asked again, bewildered.

They say that drowning victims' lives flash through their heads. Here, with William Clark Henderson frozen in the processional, my thoughts, sunk in revelations, sought answers, found none. Were there families worldwide with similar thoughts, plans, dreams locked in mirror-image flesh? Was there a genetic plot to seize the future? Would a day dawn when these unseen, unrecognized fathers, brothers, nephews, cousins rose as rulers? Or was this just God's ghost and spirit, his Providence, his unfathomable Will? Were we all identical seeds hurled forth in wide broadcasts so as not to collide?

Were we then in some broad and incalculable fashion, brother to wolves, birds, and antelope, all inked, spotted, colored the same, year on year and generation on generation back as far as minds could see? To what purpose? To economize on genes and chromosomes? Why? Would the faces of this Family, grown apart, vanish by 2001? Or would the replicas increase to envelop all cousined flesh? Or was it just a miracle of mere existence, misunderstood by two stunned fools shouting across blind generations on a summer's graduation day?

All this, all this exploded light dark, light dark across my gaze.

"What's going on?" the other me repeated.

For the line of young men and women was almost gone, quitting a scene where two idiots raved with two similar voices.

I said something, quietly, which he could not hear. When this is done, I thought, I must tear up the pictures, burn the notes. To continue this way, with old annuals, lost faces: *madness!* Trash it all, I thought. *Now.*

The young man's mouth trembled. I read his lips.

"*What* did you just say?" he asked.

"Nothing changes," I whispered.

Then, louder:

"Nothing changes!"

I waited to hear Kipling's words to that song of great sadness: *"Lord God of old, be with us yet. Lest we forget."*

Lest we forget.

When I saw the diploma go into the hands of William Clark Henderson—

I backed off, weeping, and ran.

That Old Dog Lying
in the Dust

They say that Mexicali has changed. They say it has many people and more lights and the nights are not so long there anymore and the days are better.

But I will not go see.

For I remember Mexicali when it was small and alone and like an old dog lying out in the dust in the middle of the road. And if you drove up and honked it just lay there and twitched its tail and smiled with its rusty brown eyes.

But most of all I remember a lost-and-gone one-ring Mexican circus.

In the late summer of 1945, with the war ending beyond the world somewhere, and tires and gas rationed, a friend called to ask if I would like to ramble down past the Salton Sea to Calexico.

We headed south in a beat-up Model A which steamed and seeped brown rust-water when we stopped in the late hot afternoon to skinny-dip in the cool irrigation canals that make the desert green along the Mexican border. That night we drove across into Mexico and ate cold watermelon in one of those palm-fringed outdoor stands where whole families gather happy and loud and spitting black seeds.

We strolled the unlit border town, barefoot, treading the soft brown talcum dust of its unpaved summer roads.

The warm dust blew us around a corner. The little one-ring Mexican circus lay there: an old tent full of moth holes and half-sewn wounds, propped up from within by an ancient set of dinosaur bones.

Two bands played.

One was a Victrola which hissed *"La Cucaracha"* from two black funeral horns buried high in the trees.

The second band was mortal flesh. It consisted of a bass-drummer who slammed his drum as if killing his wife, a tuba player sunk and crushed in brass coils, a trumpeter with a pint of sour saliva in his horn, and a trap-drummer whose effervescent palsy enabled him to gunshot everyone: musicians quick or musicians dead. Their mouth-to-mouth breathing brought forth *"La Raspa."*

To both calamities, my friend and I crossed the warm night-wind street, a thousand crickets frolicking at our pants cuffs.

The ticket-seller raved into his wet microphone. Volcanoes of clowns, camels, trapeze acrobats waited just inside to fall upon us! Think!

We thought. In a mob of young, old, well-dressed, poor, we hustled to buy tickets. At the entrance a tiny lady with great white piano-teeth fried tacos and tore tickets. Under her faded shawl, starlight spangled. I knew that soon she would shed her moth wings to become a butterfly, eh? She saw my face guess this. She laughed. She tore a taco in half, handed it to me, laughed again.

Pretending nonchalance, I ate my ticket.

Inside was a single ring around which were tiered three hundred slat-board seats cleverly built to kill the spines of plain meadow-beast folk like us. Down circling the ring stood two dozen rickety tables and chairs where sat the town aristocrats in their licorice-dark suits with black ties. There also sat their proper wives and uncomfortable children, all meticulous, all quiet as behooves the owners of the town cigar store, the town store that sells liquor, or the best car mechanic in Mexicali.

The show was to start at eight p.m. or as soon as the tent was full; by rare luck, the tent was full by eight-thirty. The extravaganzas lit their fuses. A whistle shrieked. The musicians, outside, flung down their instruments and ran.

They reappeared, some in coveralls to haul rope, others as clowns to bounce across the ring.

The ticket-seller lurched in, bringing with him the Victrola which he banged onto a band platform near the ring. In a great shower of sparks and minor explosions, he plugged it in, looked around, shrugged, spun a record, poised the needle. We could have either a live band or live acrobats and trapeze artists. We chose the latter.

The huge circus began—small.

Now a sword-swallower choked on a sword, sprayed kerosene in a gout of flame, and wandered out to applause from five small girls.

Three clowns knocked each other across the ring and bounded off to aching silence.

Then, thank God, the little woman leaped into the ring.

I knew those spangles. I sat up swiftly. I knew those vast teeth, those quick brown eyes.

It was the taco-seller!

But now she was—

The beer-keg juggler!

She rolled flat on her back. She shouted. The sword-swallower tossed a red-white-green keg. She caught it deftly with her white ballet-slippered feet. She spun it, as a John Philip Sousa record beat hell out of the tent canvas with a big brass swatter. The tiny lady kicked the whirling keg twenty feet up. By the time it fell to crush her, she was gone, running.

"Hey! *Ándale! Vamanos!* Ah!"

Out beyond in the dusting night I could see the colossal grand parade corseting itself together, girding its gouty loins. A small mob of men was leaning against what looked like an irritable camel out by the watermelon stands. I thought I heard the camel curse. I knew I saw its lips move with obscene belches. Were they or were they not slipping a stomach belt on the beast? *Did it have multiple hernias?*

But now one of the sweating rope-haulers jumped on the bandstand, crammed a red fez on his head, mouthed the trombone in a great wail. A new record trumpeted like a herd of elephants.

The great parade dusted in, led and followed by ten million crickets who had nothing else to do.

First in the parade was a donkey led by a fourteen-year-old boy in blue overalls with an Arabian Nights turban over his eyes. Then six dogs ran in, barking. I suspected that the dogs, like the crickets, had gotten tired of the nearest street corner and came every night to volunteer their services. There they were, anyway, dashing about, watching from the corners of their eyes to see if we saw them. We did. That drove them wild. They cavorted and yipped and danced until their tongues hung out their mouths like bright red ties.

This, for the first time, stirred the audience. As one, we burst into shouts and applause. The dogs went mad. They bit their tails on the way out.

Next came an old horse with a champanzee on his back, picking his nose and showing results to all. More applause from the children.

And then, the grandest part of the sultan's vast parade.

The camel.

It was a high-society camel.

Which is to say that while it was patched at the seams, needled and glued together with bits of yellow thread and old hemp, with floppy turrets, torn flanks, and bleeding gums, it nevertheless had one of those looks which say, I smell bad but you smell worse. That mask of utter disdain which only rich old women and dying dromedaries share.

My heart leaped.

Riding on the back of this beast, in charge of tinsel, was the tiny woman who had taken tickets, sold tacos, juggled beer kegs, and was now—

Queen of Sheba.

Flashing her lighthouse-smile to all, she waved a salute as she rode between the coming-and-going tides of camel-humps, jolting.

I shouted.

For, half 'round the ring, the camel, seized with an earthquake of arthritis, collapsed.

It fell as if its tendons were chopped.

With a ridiculous leer, with a grimace that begged our pardon, the camel crashed like a wall of canvas and dung.

It knocked one of the ringside tables flat. Beer bottles shattered amidst one elegant funeral-director husband, his hysterical wife, and two sons made joyous by this event which they would tell about for the rest of their lives.

The tiny lady with the big teeth, waving bravely, smiling her own pardon, went down with the ship of the desert.

Somehow she retained her seat. Somehow she was not rolled on or crushed. Pretending that nothing whatsoever was wrong, she continued to wave and smile as the various rope-haulers, trombone players, and trapeze artists, half-in half-out of their new-old disguises, ran to butt, kick, pummel, and spit on the eye-rolling beast. Meanwhile the rest of the parade circled the ring, making a wide detour around this point of collapse.

Getting the camel put back together this leg here, that joint there, and the neck, so! was like putting up an Arab tent in a hurricane. No sooner had these sweating architects established one leg and nailed it to the earth, than another leg creaked and broke apart.

The camel's humps flopped in opposite directions, wildly. The little woman stayed bravely sidesaddle. The phonograph brass-band pulsed, and at last the camel was reassembled; the great homely jigsaw of bad breath and Band-Aid–covered pelt reared up to shamble, walking wounded, drunk and disorderly, threatening to crack yet other tables flat, one last time around the ring.

The tiny lady way up there on the smelly dune of beast waved a final time. The audience cheered. The parade limped out. The trombone player rushed over to the platform to shut the fanfare off.

I found that I was standing, my mouth open and aching, my lungs raw with shouts of encouragement I had not heard myself give. I saw that there were dozens of others, like myself, who had been caught up in the despair of the woman and the embarrassment of the camel. Now we all sat down, giving each other quick proud looks, glad for happy endings. The band shuffled back in, wearing gold epaulettes on their work-coveralls. They struck a brass note.

"The Great Lucretia! The Butterfly of Berlin!" cried the ringmaster, appearing for the first time by the very proper tables, his trumpet hidden behind his back. "Lucretia!"

Lucretia danced out.

But of course it was not just Lucretia who danced, but tiny Melba and Roxanne and Ramona Gonzales. With many hats, many costumes, she ran with the same vast piano smile. Oh, Lucretia, Lucretia, I thought.

O woman who rides camels that fail, O woman who juggles kegs and rips tacos—

O woman, I added, who tomorrow will drive one of those flimsy tin locust-scourge trucks across the Mexican desert toward some lonely town inhabited by 200 dogs, 400 cats, 1,000 candles, and 200 forty-watt bulbs, plus 400 people. And of those 400 people, 300 will be old women and old men, 80 will be children and 20 young women waiting for young men who will never come back from across the desert where they have vanished toward San Luis Potosí, Juárez, and sea-bottoms dry and empty and baked to salt. And here comes the circus, packed in a few grasshopper-plague cars, flicking, rattling, jouncing over the pothole roads, squashing tarantulas to strawberry phlegm, crushing slow dogs to tarpaulin papier-mâché shapes left to flake at high noon on an empty turnpike, and the circus, not looking back, gone.

And this small woman, I thought, why, she is almost the whole thing. If *she* ever dies . . .

Ta-ta! said the orchestra, calling me back from reveries of dust and sun.

A silver buckle flew down out of the tent sky on a fishing line. It had come to fish for—*her!*

She attached the silver buckle to her smile.

"Oh my God, look!" said my friend. "She . . . she's going to—*fly!*"

The tiny woman with the biceps of a truck driver and the legs of a six-day bike-rider jumped.

God, on his long fishing line, drew her whizzing into the brown flapping-tent sky.

The music soared with her.

Applause shattered the air.

"How high would you say she is?" whispered my friend.

I would not answer. Twenty feet, maybe twenty-five.

But somehow, with this tent and these people and this night, it seemed a hundred.

And then, the tent began to die. Or rather the Smile began to collapse the tent.

Which is to say, the teeth of the tiny woman attached to the silver buckle pulling one way, toward the center of the earth, caused all the tent-poles to groan. Wire hummed. The canvas boomed like a drum.

The audience gasped and stared.

The Butterfly spun and whirled in her bright unfurled cocoon.

But the ancient tent gave up. Like a hairy mammoth despairing of his bones, the tent leaned, wishing to roll over and sleep.

The men holding to the rope, which had yanked the Smile, the Teeth, and Head, the Body of the brave little muscled woman fifteen and then twenty feet into the air, these men now also gazed up in terror. The poles would crush, the canvas smother their insignificant lives. Their eyes flicked to the ringmaster who snapped his whip and cried "Higher!" as if there was somewhere yet to go. She was almost to the top of the tent now and all the poles were vibrating, shaking, leaning. The orchestra brassed out a single note as if to summon an evil wind. The wind came. Outside in the night, a very dry Santa Ana indeed arrived, picked up the skirts of the tent, let the night peer under, blew a vast whiff of hot oven air in on us with dust and crickets, and fled.

The tent boomed its canvas. The crowd shivered.

"Higher!" cried the ringmaster, bravely. *"Finale!* The Great Lucretia!" Then he hissed in an explosive aside: "Lucy, *vamanos!"* Which translates to: "God sleeps, Lucy. Down!"

But she gave an impatient shake, twist, ripple of her entire muscled Mickey Rooney body. She shed her wings. She became an angry hornet cutting swathes. She spun faster, divesting herself of silks. The band played "Dance of the Seven Veils." She whipped off layer on layer of red, blue, white, green! With a series of amazing metamorphoses she spellbound our uplifted eyes.

"*Madre de Dios*, Lucretia!" cried the ringmaster.

For the canvas heaved, exhaled. The tent skeleton groaned. The angle-pullers, the rope-haulers shut their eyes, moaning, afraid to see that insanity in the air.

Lucy-Lucretia snapped both hands. Zap! A Mexican flag, an American flag sprang from nowhere into her fingers. Crick!

The band, seeing this, played the Mexican national anthem (four bars), and ended with Francis Scott Key (two).

The audience clapped, yelled! With luck, that midget dynamo would be down on the earth instead of the tent down on our heads! *Olé!*

The three ropemen let her drop.

She fell a full ten feet before they remembered she had no net. They seized the smoking rope again. You could smell their burning skin. Devil's fire leaped from their palms. They laughed with pain.

The little toy lady hit the sawdust, her smile still attached to the buckle. She reached up, unplucked the rope, and stood waving the two bright flags at the gone-mad crowd.

The tent, relieved of 110 pounds of mighty muscle, sighed. Through the many moth holes in the gray-brown canvas skin, I saw a thousand stars twinkling in celebration. The circus was to live for yet another day.

Pursued by a tidal wave of applause, the Smile and the tiny lady who owned it ran along the sawdust shore, gone.

Now: the finale.

Now, an act which would put out our lives, blow out our souls, destroy our sanity by its beauty, terror, weight, power, and imagination!

So said a rope-hauler over the lilyhorns!

The rope-hauler waved his trumpet. The band fell in a heap of super-induced affection upon a triumphal march.

The lion-tamer, in a banging cloud of pistol-fire, bounded into the ring.

He wore a white African hunter's helmet, a Clyde Beatty blouse and puttees, and Frank Buck boots.

He cracked a black whip. He fired his pistol to wake us up. The air was filled with an immense bloom of scent.

But under the shadow of his white helmet, and behind his fierce new mustache, I saw the face of the ticket-seller out front an hour ago, and the eyes of the ringmaster.

Another pistol crack. Ta!

The round lion-tamer's cage, hidden until now under a bright tarpaulin toward the rear of the tent, was revealed as its brilliant cover was yanked off.

The ring-attendants came trudging in, pulling a crate inside which we could smell a single lion. This they pushed up to the far side of the cage. Doors were opened. The lion-tamer leaped into the main cage, slammed the door, and fired his weapon at the open door of the lion's shadowy crate.

"Leo! *Ándale!*" cried the tamer.

The audience leaned forward.

But . . . no Leo.

He was asleep somewhere in that small portable crate.

"Leo! *Vamanos! Ándale!* Presto!" The tamer snapped in through the small crate door with his whip, like someone turning meat on a tired spit.

A big fluff of yellow mane rolled over with an irritable mumble.

"Gah!" The pistol was next fired into the deaf old lion's ear.

There was a most deliciously satisfying roar.

The audience beamed and settled back.

Leo suddenly manifested in the crate door. He blinked into the damned light. And he was—

The oldest lion I have ever seen.

It was a beast come forth from a retirement farm in the Dublin Zoo on a bleak day in December. So wrinkled was his face, it was a smashed window, and his gold was old gold left out in the long rains and beginning to run.

The lion needed glasses, this we could guess from his furious blinking and squinting. Some of his teeth had fallen out in his breakfast gruel only that morning. His ribs could be seen under his mangy pelt which had the look of a welcome mat trampled on by a billion lion-tamers' feet.

There was no more outrage in him. He was angered out. There was only one thing to do. Fire his pistol into the beast's left nostril—bang!

"Leo."

Roar! went the lion. Ah! said the audience. The drummer stirred up a storm on his snare drum.

The lion took a step. The tamer took a step. Suspense!

Then a dreadful thing . . .

The lion opened his mouth and yawned.

Then an even more dreadful thing . . .

A small boy, no more than three years old, somehow freed from his mother's clutch, left the elite table at the edge of the ring and toddled forward across the sawdust toward the monstrous iron cage. Cries filled the tent: No, no! But before anyone could move, the small boy plunged laughing forward and seized the bars.

No! came the gasp.

But worse still, the little boy shook not just two bars, but the *entire* cage.

With the littlest move of his tiny pink-brown fists, the boy threatened to topple the whole jungle edifice.

No! cried everyone silently, leaning forward, gesticulating at the boy with fingers and eyebrows.

The lion-tamer, with his whip and pistol upraised, sweated, waited.

The lion exhaled through his fangless mouth, eyes shut.

The small boy gave the bars a last rattling shake of terrible Doom.

Just as his father, in one swift run, scooped him up, half hid him under his Sunday coat, and retreated to the nearest formal table.

Bang! The audience exhaled, collapsed in relief, the lion roared, circled round after its own tail, and leaped upon a flake-painted pedestal, there to rear up on its hind feet.

By now, the shaken cage had stopped trembling.

Bang! The tamer fired into that vast yellow-sun face. The lion blazed a real scream of anguish and leaped! The tamer ran pell-mell. The lion raced. The tamer reached the cage door, with the lion not one pace behind. The audience shrieked. The tamer flung the door wide, spun, fired, bang, bang! then out, clang! and the door locked safe, he whipped his toupee off, flung his pistol to earth, cracked his whip, and smiled a smile that swallowed us all!

Roar! That's what the crowd did. On its feet, it imitated the lion-beast. Roar!

The show was over.

The two bands were playing outside in the watermelon-eating dust-blowing cricket-jumping night and the audience was going out and my friend and I sat for a long while until we were almost alone in the moth-eaten tent through which the stars moved yet new bright constellations into place and would continue to move their small strange fires during the night. The tent flapped its wings in a hot wind of ancient applause. We went out with the last of the crowd in silence.

We looked back in at the empty ring, at the high line at the tent-top where the silver buckle waited to be attached to the Smile.

I felt a taco in my hand and looked up. There before me was the tiny lady who rode disorganized camels, juggled kegs, tore tickets, and changed from moth to butterfly each night in the small sky. Her Smile was near, her eyes searched to find the cynic in me, and found but a friend. We both had hold of opposite ends of one taco. At last she let go. With my gift, I went.

Nearby, the phonograph hissed *"La Galondrina."* And there stood the lion-tamer, perspiration falling from his brow to make a suit of lights where it touched his khaki shirt. Lips pressed to his horn, eyes shut, he did not see me pass.

Under dusty trees, we turned a corner, and the circus was gone.

All night the wind blew warm up out of Mexico, taking the dry land with it. All night the crickets rained on our bungalow windowpanes.

We drove north. For weeks after, I beat the hot dust out of my clothes and picked the dead crickets out of my typewriter and luggage.

And still nights, twenty-nine years later, I hear that one-ring circus playing its two bands, one real, one hiccuping on records, a long way off on a warm Santa Ana wind, and I wake and sit up in bed, alone, and it is not there.

Someone in the Rain

Everything was almost the same. Now that the luggage was brought into the echoing damp cottage, with the raindrops still shining on it, and he had drawn the canvas over the car which was still warm and smelling of the drive two hundred miles north into Wisconsin from Chicago, he had time to think. First of all, he had been very lucky to get this same cabin, the one he and his brother Skip and his folks had rented twenty years ago, in 1927. It sounded just the same, there was the empty echo of your voice and your feet. Now, for some unaccountable reason, he was walking about barefoot, because it felt good, perhaps. He closed his eyes as he sat on the bed and listened to the rain on the thin roof. You had to take a lot of things into account. First of all, the trees were larger. You looked out of your streaming car window in the rain and you saw the Lake Lawn sign looming up and something was different and it was only now, as he heard the wind outside, that he realized what the real change was. The trees, of course. Twenty years of growing lush and high. The grass, too; if you wanted to get particular, it was the same grass, perhaps, he had lain in that long time ago, after the jump in the lake, his swimsuit still cold around his loins and around his thin small chest. He wondered, idly, if the latrine still smelled the way it did: of brass and disinfectant and old shuffling fumbling men and soap.

The rain stopped. It tapped occasionally on the house from the washing trees above, and the sky was the color and had the feel and expectancy of gunpowder. Now and again it cracked down the middle, all light; and then the crack was mended.

Linda was over in the ladies' rest room, which was just a run between the bushes and the trees and the small white cottages, a run through puddles now, he supposed, and bushes that shook like startled dogs when you passed, showering you with a fresh burst of cool and odorous rain. It was good that she was gone for awhile. He wanted to look for certain things. First there was the initial he had carved on the windowsill fifteen years ago on their last trip up for the late summer of 1932. It was a thing he would never have done with anyone about, but now, alone, he walked to the window and ran his hand over the surface. It was perfectly smooth.

Well then, he thought, it must have been another window. No. It was this room. And this cottage, no doubt of it. He felt a sudden resentment at the carpenter who had come in here some time ago and smoothed and sandpapered surfaces and taken away the immortality he had promised himself that rainy night when, locked into the house by the storm, he had busied himself with the careful initialing. Then he had said to himself, People will come by, years from now, and see this.

He rubbed his hand on the empty sill.

Linda arrived through the front door. "Oh, what a place," she cried, and she was almost soaked, her blonde hair was full of rain, and her face was wet. She looked at him with half an accusation. "So this is Wonderland. When did they build it? You'd think each house would have a toilet, but oh no! It's just a stone's throw to the toilet, where I spent two minutes trying to find the light switch, and five minutes after that batting off a big moth while I tried to wash up!"

A large moth. He straightened up and smiled. "Here." He gave her a towel. "Dry off. You'll be all right."

"I ran into a bush, look at my dress, drenched. God." She submerged into the towel, talking.

"I've got to go over to the men's room myself," he said, looking out the door, smiling at a thing that had come into his mind. "I'll be back."

"If you're not back in ten minutes, I'll send the Coast Guard—"

The door banged.

He walked very slowly, taking deep breaths. He just let the rain fall on him and he felt the wind tugging at the cuffs of his pants. That cottage there was where

Marion, his cousin, had stayed with her mother and father. God, how many nights had they crept off to the woods and sat on damp grass to tell ghost stories while looking at the lake. And get so scared that Marion would want to hold hands and then maybe kiss, just those small innocent kisses of ten- and eleven-year-old cousins, only touches, only gestures against loneliness. He could smell her now, Marion, the way she was before the nicotine got to her and the bottled perfumes got to her. She hadn't been his cousin, really now, for ten years or so, never really, since growing up. The really natural creature had been back here somewhere. Oh, Marion was mature now, and so was he to a certain degree. But all the same, the smell of maturity wasn't quite as pleasant.

He reached the men's washroom, and Christ, it wasn't changed a bit.

The moth was waiting for him.

It was a big soft fluttery white ghost of a moth, batting and whispering against the single filament bulb. It had been there twenty years, sighing and beating in the moist night air of the rest room, waiting for him to come back. He remembered his first encounter with it. He had been only eight and the moth had come at him like a powdery phantom, dusting down its horrible wings, screaming silently at him.

He had run, shrieking, out of the latrine, across the dark August grass, into his cottage. And, rather than go back to the latrine, he watered himself free of his bursting pain behind the cottage. After that, he had been sure to go to the toilet many times during the day, so he would not have to go back to the latrine to face the powdering terror.

Now he looked at the Moth.

"Hello," he said. "Been waiting long?"

It was a silly thing to say, but it was good being silly. He didn't like the look on Linda's face. He knew that the more excuses he could make in the next day or so to be out of her sight, the better for himself. He would save money on cigarettes by not being too near her. He would be very solicitous. "What if I run up for a bottle of whiskey, darling?" "Darling, I'm going down to the boat dock to pick up some bait." "Darling, Sam wants me to golf this afternoon." Linda didn't keep well in this kind of weather. There was something a little sour about her already.

The moth beat gently at his face. "You're pretty damned big," he said, suddenly feeling a return of the cool chill to his spine, where it had used to be. He hadn't been afraid in years, now he let himself be just a little, enjoyably, afraid of the white, whispering moth. It tinkled against the light bulb. He washed up, and for the hell of it looked into a booth to see if there was some of that mysterious writing he had once read as a boy. Magic words then, incomprehensible, strange. Now—nothing. "I know what you mean, now," he said. "Words. Limericks. All the magic gone."

Somehow, he caught himself in the mirror, the blurred, fuzzy mirror, and his face was disappointed. All the words had not turned out to be half as grand as he had conjured them to seem. Once they had been golden pronouncements of mystery. Now they were vulgar, short, shocks against accumulated taste.

He lingered to finish out a cigarette, not wanting quite yet to return to Linda.

When he entered the cottage, Linda looked at his shirt.

"That's your good shirt, and why didn't you put on your coat, it's all wet."

"I'll be all right," he said.

"You'll catch cold," she said. She was unpacking some things on the bed. "Boy, the bed's hard," she said.

"I used to sleep the sleep of the innocent on it," he said.

"Frankly," she said, "I'm getting old. When they put out a bed made of whipped cream, I'm bait."

"Lie down for awhile," he suggested. "We've got three hours before dinner—"

"How long will this rain go on?" she said.

"I don't know, probably just today, and then tomorrow, everything green. Boy, does it smell good after a rain."

But he was lying. Sometimes it rained for a week. And he hadn't minded it. He had run down to the gray choppy lake in the needling rain, while the sky over him, like a great gray crock overturned and storming, from time to time took on a crackle glaze of electric blue. Then the thunder knocked him off his feet. And he had swum in the lake, his head out, the lake feeling warm and comfortable, just because the air was filled with cold needles and he looked out at the pavilion where people danced nights, and the hotels with the warm long dim corridors hushed and quiet with running porters, and he looked at the cottage under the August thunder, him in the lake, paddling dog-fashion, the air like winter above. And he never wanted to come out of the lake, he wanted only to remain suspended in the warm water, until he turned purple with enjoyment.

Linda lay down on the bed. "God, what a mattress," she said.

He lay down beside her, not touching her.

The rain started again, gently, upon the cottage. It was as dark as night, but a very special feeling, because you knew it was four in the afternoon, though black, and the sun was above all the blackness, oh, very special.

At six o'clock, Linda painted a fresh mouth on. "Well, I hope the food's good," she said. It was still raining, a thumping, pounding, never-ending drop of storm upon the house. "What do we do this evening?" she wanted to know.

"Dance? There's a pavilion, cost a million dollars, built in 1929 just before the crash," he said, tying his tie. And again he was out of the room, in thought, and under the raining trees, eighteen years ago. Him and Marion and Skip, running in their rustling slickers, making a noise like cellophane, with the rain patting them all over, their faces greased with it, past the playground and the slides, along the posted road, and to the pavilion. Children were not allowed inside. They had stood outside with their faces pressed to the screen, watching the people inside, buying drinks, laughing, sitting at the tables, getting up and going out to dance on the dance floor to music that was muted and enclosed. Marion had stood there, enchanted, the light on her face. "Someday," she had said, "I'm going to be inside, and dance."

They had stood, with the rain touching around them, in the dark wet night, the rain dripping from the eaves of the pavilion. And the music had played "I Found My Love in Avalon" and things like "In Old Monterrey."

Then, after half an hour of the rain seeping into their shoes, and their noses chilling, and rain slipping into their raincoat collars, they had turned from the warm pavilion light and walked off, silently, the music fading, down the road back to their cabins.

Someone knocked on the front door. "Sam!" called a voice. "Hey, you two! Ready? Time for dinner!"

They let Sam in. "'How do we get up to the hotel?" asked Linda. "Walk?" She looked at the rain outside the door.

"Why not," said her husband. "It'd be fun. God, we never do anything anymore, you know what I mean, we never walk anywhere, if we have to go anyplace past a block we get in the car. Hell, let's put on our raincoats and march up, eh, Sam?"

"Okay with me, how about you, Linda?" cried Sam.

"Oh, walk?" she complained. "All that way? And in this rain?"

"Come off it," the husband said. "What's a little rain."

"All right," she said.

There was a rustling as they got into raincoats. He laughed a lot and whacked her on the backside and helped her buckle it up tight. "I smell like a rubber walrus," she said. And then they were out in the lane of green trees, slipping on the squelching grass, in the lane, sinking their rubbered feet into sludge mud furrows where cars came splashing by, whining in the thick wet dark.

"Oh, boy, this is swell!" he shouted.

"Not so fast," she said.

The wind blew, bending the trees, and by the look of it, it would last a week. The hotel was up the hill and they walked now, with less laughing, though he tried starting it again. It was after Linda slipped and fell that nobody said a thing, though Sam, when helping her up, tried to make a joke.

"If nobody minds, I'm hitching a ride," she said.

"Oh, be a sport," he said.

She thumbed the next car going up the hill. When the car stopped, the man in it shouted, "You all want a ride to the hotel?" But he walked on without saying a word, so Sam had to follow.

"That wasn't polite," said Sam.

Lightning stood on the sky, like a naked and new-born tree.

*   *   *

Supper was warm, but not of much taste, the coffee was thin and unpalatable and there were not many people in the dining room. It had that end-of-the-season feel, as if everybody had taken their clothes out of storage for the last time, tomorrow the world was ending, the lights would go out, and it was no use trying too hard to please anybody. The lights seemed dim, there was too much forced talk and bad cigar smoke.

"My feet are soaked," said Linda.

They went down to the pavilion at eight o'clock, and it was big and empty and echoing, with an empty bandstand, which filled slowly until at nine o'clock there were a lot of people seated at the tables, and the orchestra, a nine-piece band (hadn't it been a twenty-piece band in 1929, wondered the husband), broke into a medley of old tunes.

His cigarettes tasted damp, his suit was moist, his shoes were sopping, but he said nothing. When the orchestra played its third number, he asked Linda out on the floor. There were about seven couples out there, in the rainbow changing lights, in the vast echoing emptiness. His socks squeaked water as he walked, they were very cold.

He held Linda and they danced to "I Found My Love in Avalon," just because he had telephoned earlier to have it played. They moved quietly around the floor, not speaking.

"My feet are soaking wet," said Linda, finally.

He held on to her and kept moving. The place was

dim and dark and cool and the windows were washed with fresh rain still pouring.

"After this dance," said Linda, "we'll go to the cabin."

He didn't say yes or no.

He looked across the shining floor, to the empty tables, with a few couples spotted here and there, beyond them, to the watery windows. As he moved Linda across the floor, nearer to the window, he squinted, and there they were.

Outside the window, a few child faces, peering in. One or two. Perhaps three. The light on their faces. The light shining in their eyes. Just for a minute or so.

He said something.

"What'd you say?" asked Linda.

"I said I wish I were outside the window now, looking in," he said. She looked at him. The music was ending. When he looked at the window again, the faces were gone.

Madame et
Monsieur Shill

It was while shuttling his eye down the menu posted in a nineteenth-century silver frame outside Le Restaurant Fondue that Andre Hall felt the merest touch at his elbow.

"Sir," said a man's voice, "you look to be hungry."

Andre turned irritably.

"What makes you think—?" he began, but the older man interrupted, politely.

"It was the way you leaned in to read the menu. I am Monsieur Sault, the proprietor of this restaurant. I know the symptoms."

"My God," said Andre. "*That* made you come out?"

"Yes!" The older man examined Andre's coat, the worn cuffs, the too-often-cleaned lapels and said, "*Are you hungry?*"

"Do I sing for my supper?"

"No, no! *Regardez* the window."

Andrew turned and gasped, shot through the heart.

For in the window sat the most beautiful young woman, bent to ladle her soup to a most *delicious* mouth. Bent, as if in prayer, she seemed not to notice their tracing her profile, her mellow cheeks, her violet eyes, her ears as delicate as seashells.

Andre had never dined on a woman's fingers, but now the urge overwhelmed him as he fought to breathe.

"All you must do," whispered the proprietor, "is sit in that window with the lovely creature and eat and drink during the next hour. And return another night to dine with the same lovely vision."

"Why?" said Andre.

"*Regardez.*" The old man turned Andre's head so he might gaze at himself in the window's reflection.

"What do you see?"

"A hungry art student. Myself! And . . . not bad-looking?"

"Ah hah! Good. Come!"

And the young man was pulled through the door to sit at the table while the beautiful young woman laughed.

"What?" he cried, as champagne was poured. "What's so funny?"

"You," the beauty smiled. "Hasn't he said why we're here? Behold, our audience."

She pointed her champagne glass at the window where people now lingered outside.

"Who are they?" he protested. "And *what* do they see?"

"The actors." She sipped her champagne. "The beautiful people. Us. My fine eyes, nose, fine mouth, and *look* at you. Eyes, nose, mouth, *all* fine. Drink!"

The proprietor's shadow moved between them. "Do you know the magician's theater where a volunteer who is the magician's assistant *pretends* innocence to secretly help the sorcerer, eh? And the *name* of such assistants? *Shill.* So, seated with a proper wine and your audience beyond the window, I now dub thee . . ."

He paused.

"Shill. Madame *et* Monsieur . . . Shill."

And indeed as the lovely creature across from Andre raised her glass, in the twilight hour beyond the window, passersby hesitated and were pleasured by the incredible beauty and a man as handsome as she was lovely.

With a murmuring and shadowing the couples, lured by more than menus, filled the tables and more candles were lit and more champagne poured as Andre and his love, fascinated with each other's immortal faces, devoured their meal without seeing it.

So the last plates were cleared, the last wine tasted, the last candles extinguished. They sat, staring at one another, until the proprietor, in the shadows, raised his hands.

Applause.

"Tomorrow night," he said. "*Encore?*"

*   *   *

Encore and another after that and still another followed with their arrivals and departures, but always they met in silence to cause the room's temperature to change. People entering from the cool night found summer on this hearth where he fed on her warmth.

And it was in the midst of the sixteenth night that Andre felt a ventriloquist's ghost in his throat move his mouth to say:

"I love you."

"Don't!" she said. "People are watching!"

"They've been watching for weeks. They see two lovers."

"Lovers? No. We're not!"

"Yes! Come back to my room or let me come to *yours!*"

"That would spoil it! This is perfect *now.*"

"*Being* with you would be perfect."

"Sit! Look at all the people we make happy. Consider Monsieur Sault, whose future we assure. Think: before you arrived last month, what were your plans for next year? Drink the wine. They say it's excellent."

"Because they *say* it's excellent?"

"Careful. The people outside might read lips and leave. Give me your hand. *Gently!* Eat. Smile. Nod your head. There. Better?"

"I love you."

"Stop or I'll go!"

"Where?"

"Somewhere!" She smiled her false smile for the

people beyond the window. "Where working conditions are better."

"Am *I* a bad working condition?"

"You endanger us. See, Monsieur Sault glares! Be still. Pour the wine. Yes?"

"Yes," he said at last.

And so it went for another week until he burst out and said, "Marry me!"

She snatched her hand from his. "No!" Then, because a couple had paused at their window, she laughed.

"Don't you love me a little bit?" he pleaded.

"Why should I? There were no promises."

"Marry me!"

"Monsieur Sault!" she cried. "The check!"

"But there has never *been* a check!"

"Tonight," she said, "there *is*."

The next night she vanished.

"You," cried Monsieur Sault. "You fiend! Look what you've done!"

Inside the window there was no beautiful young woman: the last night of spring, the first night of summer.

"My business is ruined!" cried the old man. "Why couldn't you have shut your mouth and eaten your pâté or drunk a second bottle and stuck the cork in your teeth?"

"I told the truth as I felt it. She'll come back!"

"So? Read *this!*"

Andre took the note the old man gave him and read: *Farewell.*

"Farewell." Tears leaked from Andre's eyes. "Where's she gone?"

"God knows. We never knew her real name or address. Come!"

Andre followed up through a labyrinth of stairs to the roof. There, swaying as if he might pitch headlong down, Monsieur Sault pointed across the twilight city.

"What do you see?"

"Paris. Thousands of buildings."

"And?"

"Thousands of restaurants?"

"Do you truly know how many there are between here, the *Tour Eiffel,* and there, Notre-Dame? Twenty thousand restaurants. Twenty thousand hiding places for our nameless wonder. Would you find her? Search!"

"All twenty thousand restaurants?"

"Bring her and you'll be my son and partner. Come without her and I will kill you. Escape!"

Andre escaped. He ran to climb the hill to the white splendor of Sacré-Coeur and looked out at the lights of Paris drowned in the blue and gold colors of a vanished sun.

"Twenty thousand hiding places," he murmured.

And went down in search.

In the Latin Quarter across the Seine from Notre-Dame you could wander past forty restaurants in a single block, twenty on each side, some with windows where beauties might sit by candlelight, some with tables and laughing people in the open.

"No, no," Andre muttered. "Too much!" And veered off down an alley that ended at the Boulevard St. Michel where brasseries, *tabacs*, and restaurants swarmed with tourists; where Renoir women spoke wine as they drank, spoke food as they ate, and ignored this strange, haunted, searching young man as he passed.

My God, Andre thought. Must I cross and recross Paris from the Trocadero to Montmartre to Montparnasse, to find a single small theater-café window where candlelight reveals a woman so beautiful that all appetites bud, all joys, culinary and amorous, conjoin?

Madness!

What if I miss that one window, that illumination, that face?

Insane! What if in my confusion I revisit alleys already searched! A map! I must cross out where I've been.

So each night at sundown with the shades of violet and purple and magenta flooding the narrow alleys he set out with bright maps that darkened as he left. Once on the Boulevard de Grenelle he shouted his taxi to a halt and leaped out, furious. The taxi had gone too fast; a dozen cafés had flashed by unseen.

Then suddenly, in despair, he said:

"Honfleur? Deuville? Lyon?"

"What if," he continued, "she is *not* in Paris but

has fled to Cannes or Bordeaux with their thousands of restaurants! My God!"

That night he woke at three a.m. as a list of names passed through his head. Elizabeth. Michelle. Arielle. Which name to speak if at last he found her? Celia? Helene? Diana? Beth?

Exhausted, he slept.

And so the weeks passed into months and in the fourth month he shouted at his mirror:

"Stop! If you haven't found her special 'theater' this week, burn your maps! No more names or streets at midnight or dawn! Yes!"

His image, in silence, turned away.

On the ninety-seventh night of his search, Andre was moving along the Quai Voltaire when he was suddenly seized by a storm of emotion so powerful it shook his bones and knocked his heart. Voices that he heard but did not hear made him stagger toward an intersection, where he froze.

Across the narrow street under a bower of trembling leaves, there was a small audience staring at a brass-framed menu, and the window beyond. Andre stepped, as in a trance, to stand behind the people.

"Impossible," whispered Andre.

For in the candlelit window sat the most beautiful woman, the most beautiful love of his life. And across from her sat an amazingly handsome man. They were lifting glasses and drinking champagne.

Am I outside or in? Andre wondered. Is that me in there, as before, and in love? *What?*

He could only swallow his heart as, for an instant, the gaze of the beautiful young woman passed over him like a shadow and did not return. Instead she smiled at her friend across the candlelit table. Stunned, Andre found the entryway and stepped in to move and stand close by the couple who whispered and laughed quietly.

She was more beautiful than in all the nights he had imagined her multitudinous names. Her travels across Paris had colored her cheeks and brightened her incredible eyes. Even her laughter was made rich by a passage of time.

Outside the restaurant window, a new audience watched as Andre said:

"Excuse."

The beautiful young woman and the handsome man looked up. There was no remembrance in her eyes, nor did her lips smile.

"Madame *et* Monsieur Shill?" Andre asked, numbly.

They held hands and nodded.

"Yes?" they said.

And finished the wine.

The Mirror

Good Lord, there must be a thousand ways to tell of these two ladies. When they were girls, in yellow dresses, they could stand and comb their hair looking at each other. If life was a great Swiss clock, then these were the sprightliest cuckoos that ever jumped out of two doors at once, announcing the exact same time, each of them, not a second lost between. They blinked as if one cord was pulled by a great magician hidden behind the scenes. They wore the same shoes, tilted their heads in the same direction, and trailed their hands like white ribbons on the air as they floated by. Two bottles of cool milk, two new Lincoln pennies were never more the same. Whenever they entered the school proms the dancers halted as if someone had suddenly removed all of the air from the ballroom; everyone gasped.

"The twins," everyone said. Not a name was mentioned. What matter if their name was Wycherly; the parts were interchangeable, you didn't love one, you loved a corporative enterprise. The twins, the twins, how they floated down the great river of years, like two daisies tossed upon the waters.

"They'll marry the kings of the world," people said.

But they sat upon their porch for twenty years, they were as much a part of the park as the swans, you saw their faces uplifted and thrust forward like winter ghosts in the dark night of the film theater.

Oh, once there'd been men, or a man in their life. The word "life" is suggested because a plural noun would not do justice to their oneness. A man had tipped his hat to them here or there, only to have the hat returned to him as he was floated to the door. "Twins is what we're looking for!" you could hear the older sister saying across the twilight lawns. "We've two of everything in the house, beds, shoes, sun-chairs, dark glasses; and now how wonderful if we could find twins like ourselves, for only twins would understand what it is to be an individual and a mirror reflection—"

The older sister. Born nine minutes before the younger, and the divine right of elegant queens in her veins. "Sister do this, sister do that, sister do the other thing!"

"I'm the mirror," said Julia, the youngest, at the age of twenty-nine. "Oh, I've always known. Coral, everything went to her, the sense, the tongue, the mind, the coloring . . ."

"Alike as two vanilla cones, both of you."

"No, you don't see what I see. My pores are larger

and my skin redder and my elbows are rough. Coral says sandpaper is talcum by comparison. No, she's the person, and I only stand here and act out what she is and what she does, like a mirror, but always knowing I'm not real, I'm only so many waves of light, an optical illusion. Anyone who hit me with a rock would have seven years bad luck."

"Both of you will be married come spring, no doubt, no doubt *of* it!"

"Coral maybe, not me. I'll just go along to talk evenings when Coral has a headache and make the tea, that's a natural-born gift I have, making tea."

In 1934 there was a man, the town remembers, and not with Coral at all, but with the younger Julia.

"It was like a siren, the night Julia brought her young man home. I thought the tannery had gone down in flames. Came out on my front porch half-dressed with shock. And there was Coral on the front porch making a spell on the young man across half the lawn, and asking the earth to swallow her, and Julia hidden inside the screen door, and the young man just standing there with his hat on the wet grass. The next morning I saw Julia sneak out and grab it and run in. After that, didn't see the twins for, well, a week, and after that, there they were, sailing like boats again, down the sidewalk, the two of them, but after that I always knew which was Julia—yes, you could tell every year after that which was Julia by looking in her face."

Only last week they turned forty, the old and the young Wycherly. There must have been something about that day which broke a harp-thread so quick and so loud you could hear the clear sound of it across town.

On that morning, Julia Wycherly awoke and did not comb her hair. At breakfast the oldest one looked in her faithful mirror and said, "What's the matter with your comb?"

"Comb?"

"Your hair, your hair, it's a bird's nest." The older put her delicate porcelain hands to her own coiffure which was like gold spun and molded to her regal head, not a plait ajar, not a strand afloat, not so much as a fleck of lint or a fragment of microscopic flesh in sight. She was so clean she smelled of alcohol burning in a brass bowl. "Here, let me fix it." But Julia rose and left the room.

That afternoon another thread broke.

Julia went downtown alone.

People on the street did not recognize her. After all, you do not recognize one of a pair when for forty years you've seen only the two, like a couple of dainty shoes promenading in the downtown store-window reflections. People everywhere gave that little move of the head which meant they expected to shift their gaze from one image to its painstaking duplicate.

"Who's there?" asked the druggist, as if he'd been wakened at midnight and was peering out the door. "I mean, is that you, Coral, or Julia? Is Julia or Coral sick, Julia? I mean—damn it!" He talked in a loud voice as if a phone connection was giving him trouble. "Well?"

"This is—" The younger twin had to stop and feel herself, and see herself in the gleaming side of the apothecary vat which held green mint-colored juice in it. "This is Julia," she said, as if returning the call. "And I want, I want—"

"Is Coral dead, my God, how horrible, how terrible!" cried the druggist. "You poor child!"

"Oh, no, she's home. I want, I want—" She moistened her lips and put out a hand like vapor on the air. "I want some red tint for my hair, the color of carrots or tomatoes, I guess, the color of wine, yes, wine; I think I'd like that better. Wine."

"Two packages, of course."

"What, what?"

"Two packages of tint. One for each of you?"

Julia looked as if she might fly off, so much milkweed, and then she said, "No. Only one package. It's for me. It's for Julia. It's for Julia all by herself."

"Julia!" screamed Coral at the front door as Julia came up the walk. "Where've you been? Running off, I thought you'd been killed by a car, or kidnapped or some horrible thing! Good God!" The older sister stopped and fell back against the side of the porch rail. "Your hair, your lovely golden hair, thirty-nine inches it was, one for every year almost, one for every year." She stared at the woman who waltzed and curtsied and turned on the front lawn sidewalk, her eyes closed. "Julia, Julia, Julia!" she shrieked.

"It's the color of wine," said Julia. "And oh my it *has* gone to my head!"

"Julia, the sun, you went without your hat, and no lunch, you ate no lunch, it stands to reason. Here, let me help you in. We'll go to the bathroom and wash out that terrible color. A clown for the circus, that's what you are!"

"I'm Julia," said the younger sister. "I'm Julia, and look—" She snatched open a parcel she carried beneath her arm. She held up a dress as bright as the grass of summer, green to complement her hair, green like the trees and green like the eyes of every cat on back to the pharaohs.

"You know I can't wear green," said Coral. "Wasting our heritage money, buying dresses like that."

"One dress."

"One dress?"

"One, one, one," said Julia quietly, smiling. "One." She went in to put it on, standing in the hall. "And one pair of new shoes."

"With open toes! How ridiculous!"

"You can buy a pair just like them if you want."

"I will *not!*"

"And a dress like this."

"Ha!"

"And now," said Julia, "it's time for tea, we're due at the Applemans', remember? Come along."

"You're not serious!"

"Tea is so nice, and it's a lovely day."

"Not until you rinse your hair!"

"No, no, and I might even let it grow out, in the next six months, all gray."

"Shh, the neighbors," cried Coral, then, lower: "Your hair's not gray."

"Yes, gray as a mouse, and I'll let it grow out, we've been coloring it for years."

"Only to bring out the natural highlights, the highlights!"

They went off to tea together.

Things went quickly after that: after one explosion, another, another, another, a string, a bunch of ladyfinger firecracker explosions. Julia bought floppy flowered hats, Julia wore perfume, Julia got fat, Julia turned gray, Julia went out alone nights, pulling on her gloves like a workman approaching a fascinating job at the foundry.

And Coral?

"I'm nervous," said Coral. "Nervous, nervous, nervous. Look at her stockings, all runs. Look at her smeared lipstick, and us always neat as pins, look at her cheeks, no powder over the freckles, and her hair all dirty snow; nervous, nervous, nervous, oh, I'm nervous.

"Julia," she said at last, "the time's come. I won't be seen with you anymore.

"Julia," she said, a month later, "I've got my bags packed. I've taken room and board at Mrs. Appleman's, where you can call me if you need me. Oh, you'll call, you'll come sniveling, alone, and it'll be a long night of talking to get me home."

And Coral sailed away like a great white skiff across the sea of summer afternoon.

There was a thundershower next week. The largest single bolt of green-bolt lightning jumped around in the sky, picked its spot, and rammed itself feet-first into the center of the town, shaking birds from their nests in insane confettis, launching three children into the world two weeks ahead of time, and short-circuiting a hundred conversations by women in storm-darkened homes in mid-gallop on their way through sin and torment and domestic melodrama. This thunderbolt which jumped back up at the sky in a billion fragments was nothing to the following morning's item in the paper which said that Henry Crummitt (the man with his arm around the shoulder of the cigar-store wooden Indian) was marrying one Julia Wycherly on that self-same day.

"Someone marry Julia!"

And Coral sat down to gasp and laugh and then gasp again at the incredible lie.

"What? With her ragged seams and her dirty linens, and her awful white hair and her unplucked brows and her shoes run over? Julia? Someone take Julia to the license bureau? Oh, oh!"

But just to satisfy her humor which veered wildly between comedy and sheer slapstick which was not funny at all, she went round to the little church that afternoon and was startled to see the rice in the air and the handful of people all shouting and laughing, and there, coming out of the church, was Henry Crummitt and linked to his arm . . .

A woman with a trim figure, a woman dressed in taste, with golden hair beautifully combed, not a fleck of lint or a scrap of dandruff visible, a woman with neat stocking seams and well-delineated lipstick and powder on her cheeks like the first cool fall of snow at the beginning of a lovely winter.

And as they passed, the younger sister glanced over and saw her older sister there. She stopped. Everyone stopped. Everyone waited. Everyone held their breaths.

The younger sister took one step, took two steps forward and peered into the face of this other woman in the crowd. Then, as if she were making up in a mirror, she adjusted her veil, smoothed her lipstick, and refurbished her powder, delicately, carefully, and with no trace of hurry. Then, to this mirror she said, or it was reliably passed on she said:

"I'm Julia; who are *you?*"

And after that there was so much rice nobody saw anything until the cars had driven off.

End of Summer

One. *Two.* Hattie's lips counted the long, slow strokes of the high town clock as she lay quietly on her bed. The streets were asleep under the courthouse clock, which seemed like a white moon rising, round and full, the light from it freezing all of the town in late summer time. Her heart raced.

She rose swiftly to look down on the empty avenues, the dark and silent lawns. Below, the porch swing creaked ever so little in the wind.

She saw the long, dark rush of her hair in the mirror as she unknotted the tight schoolteacher's bun and let it fall loose to her shoulders. Wouldn't her pupils be surprised, she thought; so long, so black, so glossy. Not too bad for a woman of thirty-five. From the closet, her hands trembling, she dug out hidden parcels. Lipstick, rouge, eyebrow pencil, nail polish. A pale blue negligee, like a breath of vapor. Pulling off her cotton nightgown, she stepped on in, hard, even while she drew the negligee over her head.

She touched her ears with perfume, used the lipstick on her nervous mouth, penciled her eyebrows, and hurriedly painted her nails.

She was ready.

She let herself out into the hall of the sleeping house. She glanced fearfully at three white doors. If they sprang open now, then what? She balanced between the walls, waiting.

The door stayed shut.

She stuck her tongue out at one door, then at the other two.

She drifted down the noiseless stairs onto the moonlit porch and then into the quiet street.

The smell of a September night was everywhere. Underfoot, the concrete breathed warmth up along her thin white legs.

"I've always wanted to do this." She plucked a blood rose for her black hair and stood a moment smiling at the shaded windows of her house. "You don't know what I'm doing," she whispered. She swirled her negligee.

Down the aisle of trees, past glowing street lamps, her bare feet were soundless. She saw every bush and fence and wondered, "Why didn't I think of this a long time ago?" She paused in the wet grass just to feel how it was, cool and prickly.

The patrolman, Mr. Waltzer, was wandering down Glen Bay Street, singing in a low, sad tenor. As he passed, Hattie circled a tree and stood staring at his broad back as he walked on, still singing.

When she reached the courthouse, the only noise was the sound of her bare toes on the rusty fire escape. At the top of the flight, on a ledge under the shining silver clock face, she held out her hands.

There lay the sleeping town!

A thousand roofs glittered with snow that had fallen from the moon.

She shook her fists and made faces at the town. She flicked her negligee skirt contemptuously at the far houses. She danced and laughed silently, then stopped to snap her fingers in all four directions.

A minute later, eyes bright, she was racing on the soft lawns of the town.

She came to the house of whispers.

She paused by a certain window and heard a man's voice and a woman's voice in the secret room.

Hattie leaned against the house and listened to whispering, whispering. It was like hearing two tiny moths fluttering gently inside on the window screen. There was a soft, remote laughter.

Hattie put her hand to the screen above, her face the face of one at a shrine. Perspiration shone on her lips.

"What was that?" cried a voice inside.

Like mist, Hattie whirled and vanished.

When she stopped running she was by another house window.

A man stood in the brightly lighted bathroom, perhaps the only lighted room in the town, shaving carefully around his yawning mouth. He had black hair and blue eyes and was twenty-seven years old and every morning carried to his job in the railyards a lunch bucket packed with ham sandwiches. He wiped his face with a towel and the light went out.

Hattie waited behind the great oak in the yard, all film, all spiderweb. She heard the front door click, his footsteps down the walk, the clank of his lunch pail. From the odors of tobacco and fresh soap, she knew, without looking, that he was passing.

Whistling between his teeth, he walked down the street toward the ravine. She followed from tree to tree, a white veil behind an elm, a moon shadow behind an oak. Once, he whirled about. Just in time she hid from sight. She waited, heart pounding. Silence. Then, his footsteps walking on.

He was whistling the song "June Night."

The high arc light on the edge of the ravine cast his shadow directly beneath him. She was not two yards away, behind an ancient chestnut tree.

He stopped but did not turn. He sniffed the air.

the night wind blew her perfume over the ravine, as she had planned it.

She did not move. It was not her turn to act now. She simply stood pressing against the tree, exhausted with the shaking of her heart.

It seemed an hour before he moved. She could hear the dew breaking gently under the pressure of his shoes. The warm odor of tobacco and fresh soap came nearer.

He touched one of her wrists. She did not open her eyes. He did not speak.

Somewhere, the courthouse clock sounded the time as three in the morning.

His mouth fitted over hers very gently and easily.

Then his mouth was at her ear and she was held to the tree by him. He whispered. So *she* was the one who'd looked in his windows the last three nights! He kissed her neck. She, *she* had followed him, unseen, last night! He stared at her. The shadows of the trees fell soft and numerous all about, on her lips, on her cheeks, on her brow, and only her eyes were visible, gleaming and alive. She was lovely, did she know that? He had thought he was being haunted. His laughter was no more than a faint whisper in his mouth. He looked at her and made a move of his hand to his pocket. He drew forth a match, to strike, to hold by her face, to see, but she took his hand and held it and the unlit match. After a moment, he let the matchstick drop into the wet grass. "It doesn't matter," he said.

She did not look up at him. Silently he took her arm and began to walk.

Looking at her pale feet, she went with him to the edge of the cool ravine and down to the silent flow of the stream, to the moss banks and the willows.

He hesitated. She almost looked up to see if he was still there. They had come into the light, and she kept her head turned away so that he saw only the blowing darkness of her hair and the whiteness of her arms.

He said, "You don't have to come any further, you know. Which house did you come from? You can run back to wherever it is. But if you run, don't ever come back; I won't want to see you again. I couldn't take any more of this, night after night. Now's your chance. Run, if you want!''

Summer night breathed off her, warm and quiet.

Her answer was to lift her hand to him.

Next morning, as Hattie walked downstairs, she found Grandma, Aunt Maude, and Cousin Jacob with cold cereal in their tight mouths, not liking it when Hattie pulled up her chair. Hattie wore a grim, high-necked dress, with a long skirt. Her hair was a knotted, hard bun behind her ears, her face was scrubbed pale, clean of color in the cheeks and lips. Her painted eyebrows and eyelashes were gone. Her fingernails were plain.

"You're late, Hattie," they all said, as if an agreement had been made to say it when she sat down.

"I know." She did not move in her chair.

"Better not eat much," said Aunt Maude. "It's eight-thirty. You should've been at school. What'll the superintendent say? Fine example for a teacher to set her pupils."

The three stared at her.

Hattie was smiling.

"You haven't been late in twelve years, Hattie," said Aunt Maude.

Hattie did not move, but continued smiling.

"You'd better go," they said.

Hattie walked to the hall to take down her green umbrella and pinned on her ribboned flat straw hat.

They watched her. She opened the front door and looked back at them for a long moment, as if about to speak, her cheeks flushed. They leaned toward her. She smiled and ran out, slamming the door.

Thunder in the Morning

At first it was like a storm, far away, a touch of thunder, a kind of wind and a stirring. The streets had been emptied by the courthouse clock. People had looked at the great white clock face hours ago, folded their newspapers, got up from the porch swings, hooked themselves into their summer night houses, put out the lights, and settled into cool beds. All this the clock had done, just standing above the courthouse green. Now there was not a thing on the street. Overhead street lights, casting down illumination, made shines upon the asphalt. On occasion a leaf would break loose from a tree and clatter down. The night was so dark you could not see the stars. Why this was so there was no way of telling. Except that everyone's eyes were closed and that way no stars were seen, that's how dark the night was. Oh, here and there, behind a window screen, if one peered into a dark room, one might see a red point of light, nothing else; some man sitting up to feed his insomnia with nicotine, rocking in a slow rocker in the dark room. You might hear a small cough or someone turn under the sheets. But on the street there was not even a policeman swinging along with his club pointed to the earth in one hand.

From far away the small thunder began. First it was far across town. You could hear it across the ravine, going along the street over there, three blocks away across the deep blackness. It took a direction, it made square cuts, this sound of thunder, then it crossed over the ravine on the Washington Street bridge, under the owl light, and turned a corner and—there it was, at the head of the street!

And with a whiskering, brushing, sucking noise down the street between the houses and trees came the thundering metal cleaning machine of Mr. Britt. It was a tornado, funneling, driving, whispering, murmuring, feeling of the street ahead of it with big whirl-around brushes like sewer lids with rotary brushes under them, spinning, with a big rolling-pin brush turning under all the scattered trivia of the world's men, the ticket stubs from that show at the Elite tonight, and the wrapper from a chewing gum stick that now rested on top of a bureau in one of the houses, a small chewed cannonball of tasteless elasticity, and the candy wrapper from a bar now hidden and folded into the small accordion innards of a boy high in a cupola house in a magic room. All these things, streetcar trransfers to Chessman Park, to Live Oak Mortuary, to North Chicago, to Zion City, giveaway handbills on hairdos at that new chromium shop on Central. All these were whiskered up by the immense moving mustache of the machine, and on top of the machine, like a great god, in his leather-metal saddle, sat Mr. Roland Britt, age thirty-seven, the strange age between yesterday and tomorrow, and he, in his way, was a duplicate of the machine upon which he rode, with his proud hands on the steering wheel. He had a little curly mustache over his mouth, and little curly hairs that seemed to rotate upon his scalp under the passing lamps, and a little sucking nose that was continually astonished with the world, sucking it all in and blowing it out the astonished mouth. And he had hands that were always taking things and never giving at all. He and the machine, very much the same. They hadn't begun that way. Britt had never *started* to be like the machine. But after you rode it awhile it got up through your rump and spread through your system until your digestion roiled and your heart spun like a small pink top in you. But, on the other hand, neither had the machine intended being like Britt. Machines change also, and become like their masters, in imperceptible ways.

The machine was gentler than it used to be under an Irishman named Reilly. They sailed down the midnight streets together, through little streams of water ahead of them to dampen the trivia before combing it into its gullet. It was like a whale, with a mouth full of bristle, swimming in the moonlight seas, slaking in ticket minnows and gum-wrapper minnows, feeding and feeding in the silvery school of confetti that lived in the shallows of the asphalt river. Mr. Britt felt like a Greek god, even with his concave chest, bringing gentle April showers with him with the sprinklers, cleansing the world of dropped sin.

Halfway up Elm Road, whiskers bristling, great mustache hungrily eating of the street, Mr. Britt, in a fit of sport, swerved his great storm machine from one side of the street to the other, just so he could suck up a rat.

"Got him!"

Mr. Britt had seen the large running gray thing, leprous and horrible, skittering across under a lamp flare. Whisk! And the foul rodent was now inside the machine, being digested by smothering tides of paper and autumn leaf.

He went on down the lonely rivers of night, bringing and taking his storm with him, leaving fresh-whisked and wetted marks behind him.

"Me and my magical broomstick," he thought. "Me a male witch riding under the autumn moon. A good witch. The good witch of the East; wasn't that it, from the old Oz book when I was six with whooping cough in bed?"

He passed over innumerable hopscotch squares which had been made by children drunk with happiness, they were so crooked. He sucked up red playbills and yellow pencils and dimes and sometimes quarters.

"What was that?"

He turned upon his seat and looked behind.

The street was empty. Dark trees whirled past,

swishing down branches to tap his brow, swiftly, swiftly. But in the midst of the stiff thunder he had thought he heard a cry for help, a kind of violent screaming.

He looked in all directions.

"No, nothing."

He rode on upon the whirl-away brooms.

"What!"

This time he almost fell from his saddle the cry was so apparent. He looked at the trees to see if some man might be up one, yelling. He looked at the pale streetlights, all bleached out with so many years of shining. He looked at the asphalt, still warm from the heat of the day. The cry came again.

They were on the edge of the ravine. Mr. Britt stopped his machine. The bristles still spun about. He stopped one rotary broom, then the other. The silence was very loud.

"Get me out of here!"

Mr. Britt stared back at the big metal storage tank of the machine.

There was a man inside the machine.

"What did you say?" It was a ridiculous thing to ask, but Mr. Britt asked it.

"Get me out of here, help, help!" said the man inside the machine.

"What happened?" asked Mr. Britt, staring.

"You picked me up in your machine!" cried the man.

"I what?"

"You fool; don't stand there talking, let me out, I'll suffocate to death!"

"But you couldn't possibly have gotten into the machine," said Mr. Britt. He stood first on one foot, then on another. He was very cold, suddenly. "A thing as big as a man couldn't fit in up through the vent, and anyway, the whiskers would have prevented you from behind taken in, and anyway I don't remember seeing you. When did this happen?"

There was a silence from the machine.

"When did this happen?" demanded Mr. Britt.

Still no answer. Mr. Britt tried to think back. The streets had been entirely empty. There had been nothing but leaves and gum-wrappers. There had been no man, anywhere. Mr. Britt was a thoroughly clear-eyed man. He wouldn't miss a pedestrian if one fell.

Still the machine remained strangely silent. "Are you there?" said Mr. Britt.

"I'm here," said the man inside, reluctantly. "And I'm suffocating."

"Answer me, when did you get inside the machine?" said Britt.

"A while ago," said the man.

"Why didn't you scream out then?"

"I was knocked unconscious," said the man, but there was a quality to his voice, a hesitation, a vagueness, a slowness. The man was lying. It came to Mr. Britt as a shock. "Open up the top," said the inside man. "For God's sake, don't stand there like a fool talking, of all the ridiculous inanities, a street cleaner at midnight talking to a man inside his machine, what would people think." He paused to cough violently and spit and sputter. "I'm choking to death, do you want to go up for manslaughter?"

But Mr. Britt was not listening. He was down on his knees looking at the metal equipment, at the brushes under the machine. No, it was quite impossible. That opening was only a foot across, under there, no man could possibly be poked up into it. And anyway he hadn't been going fast. And anyway the rotary brushes would have bounced a man ahead of the machine. And anyway, he hadn't *seen* a man!

He got to his feet. He noticed for the first time that the top of his forehead was all perspiration. He wiped it off. His hands were trembling. He could hardly stand up.

"Open up, and I'll give you a hundred dollars," said the man inside the machine.

"Why should you be bribing me to let you out?" said Mr. Britt. "When it is only natural that I should let you out *free*, after all, if I picked you up I should let you out, shouldn't I? And yet, all of a sudden, you start offering me money, as if I didn't *intend* to let you out, as if you knew that I might know a reason for *not* letting you out. Why is that?"

"I'm dying," coughed the man, "and you debate. God, God, man!" There was a fierce wrestling and a pounding inside. "This place in here is full of dirt and leaves and paper. I can't *move!*"

Mr. Britt stood there. "It is *not possible*," he said,

clearly and firmly, at last, "that a man could be in my machine. I know my machine. You do not belong in there. I did not ask you to be in there. It is your responsibility."

"Bend closer . . ."

"What?"

"Listen!"

He put his ear to the warm metal.

"I am here," whispered the high voice, the sweet high fading voice. "I am in here and I wear no clothes."

"What!"

He felt his hands jerk, his fingers twitch in on themselves. He felt his eyes squeeze up almost to blind him.

"I am in here and I have no clothes," said the voice. And after a long while, "Don't you want to see me? Don't you? Don't you want to see me? I'm in here now. I'm waiting . . ."

He stood by the side of the great machine for a full ten seconds. The echo of his breathing jumped off the metal a foot from his face.

"Did you hear what I said?" whispered the voice.

He nodded.

"Well then, open the lid. Let me out. It's late. Late at night. Everyone asleep. Dark. We'll be alone . . ."

He listened to his heart beating.

"Well?" said the voice.

He swallowed.

"What are you waiting for?" said the voice, lasciviously.

The sweat rolled down his face.

There was no answer. The fierce breathing that had been in the machine for a while now suddenly stopped. The thrashing stopped.

Mr. Britt leaned forward, put his ear to the machine.

He could hear nothing now but a kind of soft inner squeaking under the lid. And a sound like one hand, cut off from the body perhaps, moving, struggling by itself. It sounded like a small thing moving.

"I climbed in to sleep," said the man.

"Oh, now you *are* lying," said Mr. Britt.

He climbed up on his silent machine and sat in the leather saddle. He put his foot down to start the motor.

"What are you doing?" the voice shouted from under the lid suddenly. There was a dull stir. There was a sound as of a large body again. The heavy breathing returned. It was so sudden it made Mr. Britt almost fall from his perch. He looked back at the lid.

"No, no, I won't let you out," he said.

"Why?" cried the failing voice.

"Because," said Mr. Britt, "I have my work to do." He started the machine and the whisking thunder of the brushes and the roar of the motor drowned out the screams and shouts of the captured man. Looking ahead, eyes wet, hands hard on the wheel, Mr. Britt took his machine brooming down the silent avenues of the night town, for five minutes, ten minutes, half an hour, an hour, two hours more, sweeping and scouring and never stopping, sucking in tickets and combs and dropped soup-can labels.

At four in the morning, three hours later, he drew

up before the vast rubbish heap that slid down the hill in a strange avalanche to the dark ravine. He backed the machine up to the edge of the avalanche and for a moment cut the motor.

There was not the slightest sound from inside the machine.

He waited, but there was nothing but the beat of his heart in his wrists.

He flipped a lever. The entire cargo of branches and dust and paper and tickets and labels and leaves fell back and piled in a neat pile upon the edge of the ravine. He waited until everything had slid out upon the ground. Then he flipped the lever, slamming the lid shut, looked back once at the silent mound of rubbish, and drove off down the street.

He lived only three houses from the ravine. He drove his machine up before his house, parked, and went in to bed. He lay in the quiet room, not able to sleep, from time to time getting up and going to look out the window at the ravine. Once he put his hand on the doorknob, half opened the door, shut it, and went back to bed. But he could not sleep.

It was only at seven in the morning as he was brewing some coffee, when he heard the sound, that he knew any relief. It was the sound of young Jim Smith, the thirteen-year-old boy, who lived across the ravine. Young Jim came whistling down the street, on his way to the lake to fish. Every morning he came along in mists, whistling, and always he stopped to rummage through the rubbish left by Mr. Britt to seek dimes and quarters and orange bottle caps to pin to his shirtfront. Mr. Britt moved the window curtains aside to peer out into the early dawn mists to see little Jim Smith walk jauntily by carrying a fish pole over one shoulder, and on the end of the line at the top of the fish pole, swinging back and forth like a gray pendulum in the mists, was a dead rat.

Mr. Britt drank his coffee, crept back in bed, and slept the sleep of the victorious and innocent.

The Highest Branch on
the Tree

I often remember his name, Harry Hands, a most unfortunate name for a fourteen-year-old boy in ninth grade in junior high in 1934, or in any other year, come to think of it. We all spelled it 'Hairy' and pronounced it with similar emphasis. Harry Hands pretended not to notice and became more arrogant and smart-ass, looking down his nose at us dumb peasants, as he called us. We didn't see at the time that it was our harassment that made him pretend at arrogance and display wits that he probably only half had. So it went with Hands and his incredible moniker Hairy.

The second memory is often of his pants up a tree. That has stayed with me for a lifetime. I have never for a month forgotten. I can't very well say I recalled his pants up a tree every day, that would not be true. But at least twelve times a year I would see Harry in full flight and us ninth graders after him, myself in the lead, and his pants in the air flung up to the highest branch and everyone laughing there on the school grounds and a teacher leaning out a window and ordering one of us, why not me, to climb and bring those pants down.

"Don't bother," Harry Hands said, blushing there, revealed in his boxer BVD underwear. "They're mine. *I'll* get 'em."

And Harry Hands climbed up, almost fell, and reached his pants but did not put them on, just clutched to the bole of the tree and when we all gathered below the tree, knocking each other's elbows and pointing up and laughing, simply looked down at us with the strangest grin and . . .

Peed.

That's right.

Took aim and peed.

There was a mob flight of indignant teenagers, off away, but no one came back to climb up and drag him down, for when we started to come back, wiping our faces and shoulders with handkerchiefs, Harry yelled down:

"I had *three* glasses of orange juice for lunch!"

So we knew he was still loaded and we all stood thirty feet back from the tree yelling euphemisms instead of epithets, the way our folks had taught us. After all, it was another time, another age, and the rules were observed.

Harry Hands did not put on his pants up there nor did he come down even though the principal came out and ordered him to leave and we backed off and heard the principal shouting up at Harry that the way was clear now and he could come down. But Harry Hands shook his head: no *way*. And the principal stood under the tree and we yelled to him to watch out, Harry Hands was armed and dangerous and hearing this the principal backed off, hastily.

Well, the long and short of it was, Harry Hands never came down, that is, we didn't see him do it, and we all got bored and went home.

Someone later said he came down at sunset or midnight, with no one around to see.

The next day, the tree was empty and Harry Hands was gone forever.

He never came back. He didn't even come back to protest to the principal, nor did his parents come or write a letter to lodge a complaint. We didn't know where Harry Hands lived, and the school wouldn't tell us, so we couldn't go find him, perhaps with the faintest notion that maybe we should apologize and ask him back. We knew he wouldn't come, anyway. What we had done was so horrendous, it could never be forgiven. As the days passed and Harry Hands didn't show, most of us lay in bed at night and wondered how *we* would feel if someone had "pantsed" us and threw our pants to the highest branch of some tree in front of God and everyone. It caused a lot of unexpected bed tossing and pillow punching, I don't mind saying. And most of us didn't look up at that tree for more than a few seconds before turning away.

Did any of us ever sweat over the dire consequences? Did we perspire on the obvious that perhaps he might have fallen just at midnight, to be harvested as broken bones at dawn? Or did we imagine he might have lurched himself out in a high-jump of doom, with the same shattered consequence? Did we think his father might lose his job or his mother take to drink? We wrestled none of these or if we did, shut our traps to preserve our silent guilt. Thunder, as you know, occurs when lightning sucks back up its track and lets two handsful of white-hot air applaud. Harry Hands, whose parents were never seen, withdrew to a bang of thunder that only we ninth-grade second-rate criminals heard while waiting for sleep, which never came, to arrive.

It was a bad end to a good year and we all went off to high school and a few years later, going by the schoolyard, I saw that the tree had got some sort of disease and had been cut down, which was a relief. I didn't want some future generation to be surprised at the ghost shape of a pair of pants up there, hurled by a mob of apes.

But I run ahead of my story.

Why, you ask, why did we do that to Harry Hands? Was he some sort of super-villain who deserved our Christian persecution, a dumb sort of semi-crucifixion to appall the neighbors and ruin school history so that in the annals of time people would say, "1934, wasn't that the year that—" And fill in the blanks with Look, ma, no pants, no Hands.

What, in sum, was H.H.'s crime sublime?

It's a familiar case. Happens every year, every school, everywhere at one time or another. Except our case was more spectacular.

Harry Hands was smarter than anyone else in the whole school.

That was the first crime.

His second crime, worse than the first, was he didn't do a better job of hiding it.

It reminds me of an actor friend who a few years ago drove up to the front of my house in a brand-new super-powered XKE twelve-cylinder Jaguar and yelled at me, "Eat your heart out!"

Well, Harry Hands, in effect, had arrived at our school from somewhere back East—hadn't we all?— and flaunted his IQ from the first hour of day one. Through every class from just after breakfast to just before lunch to last afternoon bell his arm was permanently up, you could have raised a flag on it, and his voice was demanding to be heard and damn if he wasn't right when the teacher gave him the nod. A lot of collective bile was manufactured that day under all our tongues. The miracle was we didn't rip his clothes off on that first day. We delayed because it was reported that in gym he had put on the boxing gloves and bloodied three or four noses before our coach told everyone to run out and do six laps around the block to lance our boils.

And, Jesus off the cross and running rings around us, wouldn't you know as we made the fifth lap, panting, tasting blood, here came Harry Hands, fresh as a potted daisy, jogging along, nice and easy, passing us and adding another lap to prove he was tireless.

By the end of the second day he had no friends. No one even *tried* to be one. It was hinted that if anyone took up with this Hands guy, we would beat the tar out of them next time we did laps and were out of sight of our coach.

So Harry Hands came and went alone, with a look of the insufferable book reader and, worse, book rememberer, he forgot nothing and would offer data if someone paused, stuttered, or broke wind.

Did Harry Hands see his crucifixion coming? If he did, he smiled at the prospect. He was always smiling and laughing and being a good chum, although no one smiled or laughed back. We took our homework home. He did it in class in the last five minutes of the hour and then sat there, mightily pleased with his intellectual strengths, moistening his vocal chords for the next recitation.

Fade out. Fade in.

We all went away to life.

After about forty years it got so I only thought about Harry Hands once every two years instead of once every two months. It was in the middle of a sidewalk in downtown Chicago where I walked when I had two hours between trains, on my way to New York, that I met this stranger coming toward me, unrecognizable, and he had almost passed when he froze in midstride and half turned to me and said:

"Spaulding?" he said. "*Douglas* Spaulding?"

It was my turn to freeze and I mean I turned cold, for I had this ungodly feeling I was confronted by a ghost. A whole flock of geese ran over my grave. I cocked my head and eyed the stranger. He was dressed in a beautifully tailored blue-black suit with a silk shirt and a reticent tie. His hair was dark and moderately gray at the temples and he smelled of a mild cologne. He held out a well-manicured hand.

"Harry Hinds," he said.

"I don't think . . ." I said.

"You *are* Douglas Spaulding, aren't you?"

"Yes, but—"

"Berendo Junior High School, class of summer 1935, though *I* never graduated."

"Harry," I said and stopped, his last name a stone in my mouth.

"Use to be Hands. Harry Hands. Changed it to Hinds, late spring 1935—"

Jut after you climbed down, I thought.

The wind blew around one of those Chicago corners.

I smelled pee.

I glanced to left and right. No horses in sight. No dogs.

Only Harry Hinds, aka Harry Hands waiting for me to open up.

I took his fingers as if they contained electric shocks, shook them quickly, pulled back.

"My goodness," he said. "Am I still poison?"

"No, but—"

"You look well," he said quickly. "Look as if you've had a good life. That's nice."

"You, too," I said, trying not to look at his expensively manicured nails and brightly polished shoes.

"I can't complain," he said, easily. "Where are you headed?"

"The Art Institute. I'm between trains. I have almost two hours' layover and always go to the museum to look at that big Seurat."

"It is big, isn't it, and beautiful. Mind if I come partway?"

"No, no. Please, join up."

We walked and he said, "It's on the way to my office, anyway, so we'll have to talk fast. Give me your resume, for old times' sake?"

We walked and I told. Not much for there wasn't much to detail. Fair life as a writer, nicely established, no international fame but a few fans across country and enough income to raise a family. "That's it," I said. "In a nutshell. End of resume."

"Congratulations," he said and seemed to mean it, nodding. "Well done."

"What about you?" I said.

"Well," he said, reluctantly. It was the only time in all the years, then and now, I ever saw him hesitate. He was looking sidewise at a building facade which seemed to make him nervous. I glanced over and saw:

HARRY HINDS AND ASSOCIATES

FIFTH AND SIXTH FLOORS

Harry caught my gaze and coughed. "It's nothing. I didn't mean to bring you here. Just passing—"

"My God," I said. "That's quite a building. Do you own the whole thing?'

"Own it, built it," he admitted, brightening somewhat, leaning toward the old young Harry of forty years back. "Not bad, eh?"

"Not bad at all," I said, gasping.

"Well, I'd better let you get on to the Seurat," he said, and shook my hand. "But hold on. Why not? Duck inside for just sixty seconds. Then I'll let you run. Yes?"

"Why not," I said, and he took my elbow and steered me, opening the door ahead of me and bowing a nod and leading me out into the center of a spacious marble lobby, an area some sixty feet high and eighty or ninety feet across, in the center of which was an arboretum with dense jungle foliage below and a buckshot scattering of exotic birds, but with only one singular dramatic piece in the middle.

It was a single tree of some forty or fifty feet in height, but it was hard to tell what kind of tree it was, maple, oak, chestnut, what? because there were no leaves on the tree. It was not even an autumn tree with the proper yellow and red and orange leaves. It was a barren winter tree that reached for a stark sky with empty twigs and branches.

"Ain't she a beaut?" said Harry Hinds, staring up.

"Well," I said.

"Remember when old Cap Trotter, our gym coach, used to make us go out and run around the block six or seven times to teach us manners—"

"I don't recall—"

"Yes, you do," said Harry Hinds, easily, looking at the interior sky. "Well, do you know what I used to do?"

"Beat us. Pull ahead and make the six laps. Win and not breathe hard. I remember now."

"No, you don't." Harry studied the glass roof seventy feet above. "I never ran the laps. After the first two I hid behind a parked car, waited for the last lap to come around, then jumped out and beat the *hell* out of all of you."

"So *that's* how you did it?" I said.

"The secret of my success," he said. "I've been jumping from behind cars on the last lap for years."

"God damn," I whispered.

"Yeah," he said, and studied the cornices of the interior court.

We stood there for a long moment, like the pilgrims at Lourdes waiting for the daily miracle. If it happened, I was not aware. But Harry Hinds was. He pointed with his nose and eyebrows up, up along that huge tree and said, "See anything up there?"

I looked and shook my head. "Nope."

"You *sure*?" said Harry.

I looked again and shook my head.

"The highest branch on the tree?" said Harry.

"Nothing," I said.

"Funny." Harry Hinds snorted faintly. "How come I see it clearly?"

I did not ask what it was he was seeing.

I looked up at the bare tree in the middle of an arboretum in the center of the lobby of the Harold Hinds Foresight Corporation.

Did I expect to see the phantom outlines of a pair of pants way up there on the highest branch?

I did.

But there was nothing there. Only a high branch and no clothing.

Harry Hinds watched me looking at the tree and read my thought.

"Thanks," he said, quietly.

"What?" I said.

"Thanks to you, to all of you, for what you did," he said.

"What'd we do?" I lied.

"You know," he said, quietly. "And thanks. Come on."

And before I could protest, he led the way to the men's and raised his brows, nodding, did I need to go? I did.

Standing at the porcelains, unzipped, Harry looked down as he watered the daisies.

"You know," he smiled, "there isn't a day in my life, when I do this, that I don't remember that day forty years ago and me up the tree and you down below and me peeing on all of you. Not a day passes I don't remember. You, them, and peeing."

Standing there, I froze and did nothing.

Harry finished, zipped up, and stood remembering. "Happiest day of my life," he said.

A Woman Is a
Fast-Moving Picnic

The subject was women, by the singles and in the mobs.

The place was Heeber Finn's not-always-open but always-talking pub in the town of Kilcock, if you'll forgive the implication, in the county of Kildare, out along the River Liffey somewhat north and certainly beyond the reach of Dublin.

And in the pub, if only half full of men but bursting with talk, the subject was indeed women. They had exhausted all other subjects, hounds, horses, foxes, beers as against the hard stuff, lunatic mother-in-laws out of the bin and into your lives, and now the chat had arrived back to women in the pure state: unavailable. Or if available, fully dressed.

Each man echoed the other and the next agreed with the first.

"The dreadful fact is," said Finn, to keep the converse aroar, "there is no single plot of land in all Ireland which is firm or dry enough to lie down with purpose and arise with joy."

"You've touched the bull's-eye and pierced the target," said Timulty, the local postmaster, in for a quick one, there being only ten people waiting at the post-office. "There's no acre off the road, out of sight of the priest or out of mind of the wife, where physical education can be pursued without critical attention."

"The land is all bog," Nolan nailed it, "and no relief."

"There's no place to cavort," said Riordan, simply.

"Ah, that's been said a thousand times this night," protested Finn. "The thing is, what do we *do* about it?"

"If someone would only stop the rain and fire the priests," suggested Nolan.

"That'll be the day," cried all, and emptied their drinks.

"It reminds me of that Hoolihan tragedy," said Finn, refilling each glass. "Is that remembered?"

"*Say* it, Finn."

"Well, Hoolihan wandered this woman who was no Madonna, but neither was she last year's potatoes, and they passed a likely turf which seemed more flatland than swamp and Hoolihan said, Trot on out on that bog. If it holds, I'll follow. Well, she trotted out and turns around and—*sinks!* Never laid a hand on her. Before he could shout: No! she was gone!"

"The truth is," Nolan obtruded, "Hoolihan threw her a rope. But she slung it round her neck instead of her waist and all but strangled in the pulling out. But I like your version best, Finn. Anyways, they made a song of it!"

And here Nolan began, but everyone put in to finish the verse:

"The sinking of Molly in old Kelly's bog
Is writ in the Lord Mayor's roll call and a log
Poor Molly went there with the Hoolihan boy
And sank out of sight with one last shriek of joy.
He took her out there for what do you suppose?

And was busy at ridding the lass of her clothes,
But no sooner deprived of each last seam and stitch
Than she wallowed and sank and was lost in the ditch.
The ducks they all gaggled and even the hog
Wept Christian salt-tears for Moll sunk in the bog—"

"It goes on from there," said Nolan. "Needless to say the Hoolihan boy was distraught. When you're thinking one thing and another occurs, it fair turns the mind. He's feared to cross a brick road since without testing for quicksand. Shall I go on?"

"No use," cried Doone, suddenly, no more than four foot ten inches high but terrible fast plummeting out of theaters ahead of the national anthem, the local Anthem Sprinter, as everyone knows. Now, on tiptoe, he boxed the air around the pub and voiced his protest. "What's the use of all this palaver the last thousand nights when it's time to act? Even if there was a sudden flood of femininity in the provinces with no lint on them and their seams straight, what would we *do* with them?"

"True," admitted Finn. "God in Ireland just tempts man but to disown him."

"God's griefs and torments," added Riordan. "I haven't even wrestled Adam's old friend Eve late nights in the last row of the Gayety Cinema!"

"The Gayety Cinema?" cried Nolan in dread remorse. "Gah! I crept through the dark there once and found me a lass who seemed a salmon frolicking upstream. When the lights came on, I saw I had taken communion with a troll from the Liffey bridge. I ran to commit suicide with drink. To hell with the Gayety and all men who prowl there with dreams and slink forth with nightmare!"

"Which leaves only the bogs for criminal relief and drowned in the bargain. Doone," said Finn, "do you have a plan, you with that big mouth in the tiny body?"

"I have!" said Doone, not standing still, sketching the air with his fists and fingers as he danced to his own tune. "You must admit that the various bogs are the one place the Church puts no dainty toe. But also a place where a girl, representing the needy, and out of her mind, might test her will to defy the sinkage. For it's true, one grand plunge if you're not careful and no place to put her tombstone. Now hear this!"

Doone stopped so all might lean at him, eyes wide, and ears acock.

"What we need is a military strategist, a genius for

scientific research, in order to recreate the Universe and undo the maid. One word says it all. Me!"

"You!" cried all, as if struck in a collective stomach.

"I have the hammer," said Doone. "Will you hand me the nails?"

"Hang the picture," said Finn, "and fix it straight."

"I came here tonight with Victory in mind," said Doone, having slept late till noon and gone back to bed at three to adjust the sights and rearrange our future. "Now, as we waste our tongues and ruin our nervous complexions, the moon is about to rise and the empty lands and hungry bogs await. Outside this pub, in boneyards of handlebars and spokes, lie our bikes. In a grand inquest, should we not bike on out to peg and string the bogs for once and all, full of brave blood and booze, to make a permanent chart, map the hostile and innocent-looking flats, test the sinkages, and come back with the sure knowledge that behind Dooley's farm is a field in which if you do not move fast, you sink at the rate of two or three inches per minute? Then beyond, Leary's pasture in which his own cows have the devil's time grazing quick enough to survive the unsteady turf and live on the road. *Would that not be a good thing to know* for the rest of our lives so we can shun it and move to more substantial grounds?"

"My God," said all in admiration. "It *would!*"

"Then what are we waiting for?" Doone ran to the door. "Finish your drinks and mount your bikes. Do we live in ignorance or at last play in the fields, as it 'twere, of the Lord?"

"The fields!" The men drank.

"Of the Lord!" they finished, plummeting Doone out the door.

"Time!" cried Finn, since the pub was empty. "Time!"

No sooner on the road, with coattails flying as if heaven lay ahead and Lucifer behind, than Doone pointed now here, now there with his surveyor's nose:

"There's Flaherty's. Terrible quick. You're out of sight, a foot a minute and no one the wiser if they look the other way."

"Why, Christ himself," said someone in the sweating biking mob, "might not make it across!"

"He'd be the first and last and no one between!" Finn admitted, catching up with the team.

"Where are you taking us, Doone?" gasped Nolan.

"You'll see soon enough!" Doone churned his sprockets.

"And when we *get* there," asked Riordan, suddenly struck with the notion, "in the penultimate or final sinkage tests *who* will be the woman?"

"True!" gasped all, as Doone veered the path and sparked his wheels, "there's only *us*."

"Never fear!" said Doone. "One of us will *pretend* to be the poor put-upon maid, maiden, courtesan—"

"Hoor of Babylon?" volunteered Finn.

"And who would that be?"

"You're looking at his backside!" cried Doone, all elusive speed. *"Me!"*

"You!"

That almost swerved them into multiple collisions. But Doone, fearing this, cried, "And more surprises, if all goes well. Now, by God, *on* with the brakes. We're here!"

It had been raining, but since it rained all the while, no one had noticed. Now the rain cleared away like a theater curtain, to reveal:

Brannagan's off-the-road-and-into-the-woods pasture, which started in mist, to be lost in fog.

"Brannagan's!" Everyone braked to a stillness.

"Does it not have an air of the mysterious?" whispered Doone.

"It does," someone murmured.

"Do you *dare* me to be brave?"

"*Do* that," was the vote.

"But are you *serious*, Doone?"

"Jesus," said Doone. "It'll be no test for judgments and sinkage tests if someone for starters doesn't do more than jog about the territory like mindless bulls. There must be *two* people making tracks, beyond. Me, playing the woman for sure. And some volunteer amongst you."

The men inched back on their bike-seats.

"Ah, you and your scientific logic will be the death of brewing and the burial of gin," said Finn.

"But Doone, your verisimilitude, if there is such a word. It'll be hard for us to conjure you up as a female."

"Why not," offered Riordan, "go fetch a real lass here? A gal from the nunnery—"

"Nunnery!" cried all, shocked.

"Or one of the wives?" said Doone.

"Wives?" cried all, in worse shock.

And they would have driven him like a spike into the earth, had they not realized he was yanking their legs to steer them crooked.

"Enough!" Finn interjected. "Do we have pencils and paper at hand to align the sums and recall the burial sinks, plot on plot?"

The men muttered.

No one had thought to bring pencil and paper.

"Ah, hell," groused Riordan. "We'll recall the numerals, back at the pub. Out with you, Doone. In time, a volunteer, playing the male counterpart, will follow."

"Out it is!" Doone threw down his bike, doused his throat with gargle, and trotted, elbows in a grand rhythm, over the endlessly waiting and terribly damp boneyard of sexual beasts.

"This is the silliest damn thing we ever tried," said Nolan, tears in his eyes for fear of never seeing Doone again.

"But what a *hero*!" reasoned Finn. "For would we dare come here with a real crazed female if we did not know the logistics of tug and pull, devastation or survival, love-at-last as against another night of being strangled by our underwear?"

"Aw, put a sock in it!" shouted Doone, far out now, beyond rescue. "Here I go!"

"*Further* out, Doone!" suggested Nolan.

"Cripes!" cried Doone. "First you say it's a silly damn thing we do, then you instruct me to the land mines! I'm furthering by fits and starts."

Then suddenly Doone shrieked. "It's an elevator I'm in! I'm going *down!*"

He gesticulated wildly for balance.

"Off with your coat!" Finn yelled.

"What?"

"Eliminate the handicaps, man!"

"What?"

"Tear off your *cap!*"

"My cap? Nitwit! What good would *that* do?"

"Your pants then! Your shoes! You must pretend to get ready for the Grand Affair, with or without rain."

Doone kept his cap on but yanked his shoes and belabored his coat.

"The *test*, Doone!" Nolan shouted. "If you do not writhe to remove your shoelaces and untie your tie, we will not know just how fast a maid in the undressing or a man at his mating dance will slide from view. Now we must find is there or is there *not* time for a consummation devoutly to be wished?"

"Consummation—devoutly—damn!" cried Doone.

And grousing epithets and firing nouns to smoke the air, Doone danced about, flinging off his coat and then his shirt and tie and was on his way to a dropping of the pants and the rising of the moon when a thunderous voice from Heaven or an echo from the mount banged the air like a great anvil somehow fallen to earth.

"What goes *on* there?" the voice thundered.

They froze, a riot iced by sin.

Doone froze, an art statue on its way to potato deeps.

All *time* froze and again the pile-driver voice was lifted and plunged to crack their ears. The moon fled behind a fog.

"Just what in hell is going *on* here?" thundered the voice of Kingdom Come and the Last Judgment.

A dozen heads spun on a dozen necks.

For Father O'Malley stood on a rise in the road, his bike clenched in his vengeful fists, so it looked like his skinny sister, straddled and lost.

For a third time, Father O'Malley tossed the bolt and split the air. "You and you and you! What are you *up* to?"

"It's not so much up as down to my smalls," piped Doone in a wee piccolo voice, and added, meekly, "Father—"

"Out, out!" shouted the priest, waving one arm like a scythe. "Away!" he blathered. "Go, go, go. Damn, damn, damn."

And he harvested the men with maniac gesticulations and eruptions of lava enough to lay a village and bury a blight.

"Out of my sight. Away, the mangy lot of you! Go search your souls, and get your asses to confession six Sundays running and ten years beyond. It's lucky 'twas

me came on this calamity and not the Bishop, me and
not the sweet morsel nuns from just beyond Meynooth,
me and not the child innocents from yonder school.
Doone, pull up your socks!"

"They're pulled!" said Doone.

"For one last time, out!" And the men might have
scattered but they held to their bikes in deliriums of
terror and could only listen.

"Will you tell me now," intoned the priest, one eye
shut to take aim, the other wide to fix the target, "what,
what in hell are you *up* to?"

"Drowning, your lordship, your honor, your
reverence."

And this Doone almost did.

Until the monsignor was gone, that is.

When he heard the holy bike ricket away over the
hill, Doone still stood like a chopfallen Lazarus to sur-
vey his possible ruination.

But at last he called across the boggy field with a
strange frail but growing-more-triumphant-by-the-min-
ute voice:

"Is he gone?"

"He is, Doone," said Finn.

"Then look upon me," said Doone.

All looked, then stared, then gaped their mouths.

"You are not *sinking*," gasped Nolan.

"You have not *sunk*," added Riordan.

"I have *not!*" Doone stomped his foot as if to test,
then, secure, he lowered his voice for fear that the
priest, though gone, might catch the echo.

"And why not?" he asked the heavens.

"*Why*, Doone?" was the chorus.

"Because I distilled the rumors and cadged the notions that once on a time, a hundred years back, on this very spot once stood—"

He paused for the drama, then finished the act:

"A church!"

"A church?"

"Good Roman rock on uncertain Irish soil! The beauty of it distilled faith. But the weight of it sank its cornerstone. *The priests fled and left* the structure, altar and all, so it's on that firm foundation that Doone, your sprinter, holds still. I stand *above* ground!"

"It's a revelation you've made!" Finn exclaimed.

"I have! And it is here we shall conjugate our verbs and revive our faith in women in all futures, near and far," announced Doone, way out there on the rainy moss. "But just in case . ."

"In case?"

Doone waved over beyond them.

The men, straddling their bikes, turned.

And on a rise, unseen heretofore, but now half revealed to the sight, some hundred feet away, there appeared two women, not transfigured rose gardens, no, but their homely glances somehow turned fine by night and circumstance.

Short women they were. Not Irish-short but circus-short, carnival-size.

"Midgets!" exclaimed Finn.

"From the vaudeville in Dublin last week!" admitted Doone, out in the bog. "And both weighing half again less than me, should the church roof below suddenly lose its architectural roots and douse the bunch!"

Doone whistled and waved. The tiny maids, the little women, came on the run.

When they reached Doone and did not vanish, Doone called to the mob, "Will you give up your bikes and join the dance?"

There was a mass movement.

"Hold it!" cried Doone. "One at a time. We don't want to meet back at the pub at midnight—"

"And find someone *missing?*" asked Finn.

Virgin Resusitas

She sounded crazy with joy on the phone. I had to calm her down.

"Helen," I said, "take it easy. What's going on?"

"The greatest news. You must come over, now, right now."

"This is Thursday, Helen. I don't usually see you on Thursdays. Tuesdays were always it."

"It can't wait, it's too wonderful."

"Can't you tell me over the phone?"

"It's too personal. I hate saying personal things on the phone. Are you *that* busy?"

"No, I just finished up some letters."

"Well then, come and celebrate with me."

"This had better be good," I said.

"Wait till you hear. Run."

I hung up slowly and walked slowly to put on my coat and reach for my courage. There was a feeling of doom waiting outside my door. I plowed through it, made it to my car, and drove through a self-imposed silence, with an occasional curse, to Helen's apartment across town. I hesitated at knocking on her door, but it sprang open, surprising me. The look on Helen's face was so wild I thought she had come off her hinges.

"Don't just stand there," she cried. "Come in."

"It's not Tuesday, Helen."

"And never will be *again!*" she laughed.

My stomach turned to lead. I let her pull me by the elbow, lead me in, sit me down, then she whirled through the room finding wine and filling glasses. She held one out to me. I only stared at it.

"Drink," she said.

"I have a feeling it won't do any good."

"Look at me! *I'm* drinking! It's a celebration!"

"Every time you've ever used that word, part of the continent falls off into space. Here goes. What am I celebrating?"

I sipped and she touched my glass, indicating I should finish it so it could be refilled.

"Sit down, Helen. You make me nervous standing there."

"Well." She finished her glass and refilled both and sat down with a great exhalation of joy. "You'll never guess."

"I'm trying hard not to."

"Hold on to your hat. I've joined the Church."

"You—what church?" I stammered.

"Good grief! There's only *one!*"

"You have a lot of Mormon friends, and a few Lutherans on the side . . ."

"My God," she cried. "Catholic, of course."

"Since when have you liked Catholics? I thought you were raised in an Orange family, family from Cork, *laughed* at the Pope!"

"Silly. That was then, this is now. I am certified."

"Give me that bottle." I downed my second wine and refilled and shook my head. "Now, give me that again. Slowly."

"I've just come from Father Reilly's down the street."

"who—?"

"He's the head priest at St. Ignatius. He's been preparing me, you know, instruction, the last month or so."

I fell back in my chair and peered into my empty glass. "Is *that* why I didn't see you last week?"

She nodded vigorously, beaming.

"Or the week before or the week before *that?*"

Again a wild nodding agreement, plus a burst of laughter.

"This Father Kelly—"

"Reilly."

"Reilly, Father. Where did you meet him?"

"I didn't exactly meet him." She glanced at the ceiling. I looked up to see what was there. She saw me looking and glanced back down.

"Well, bumped into him, then," I inquired.

"I—well, hell. I made an *appointment*."

"A fallen-away-long-time-ago Cork-energized *Baptist* maid?"

"Don't get in an uproar."

"This is not an uproar. It's a former lover trying to comprehend . . ."

"You're *not* a former lover!"

She reached out to touch my shoulder. I looked at her hand and it fell away.

"What am I, then? An *almost* former?"

"Don't *say* that."

"Maybe I should let *you* say it. I can see it in your mouth."

She licked her lips as if to erase the look.

"How long ago did you meet, bump, make an appointment with Reilly?"

"*Father* Reilly. I dunno."

"Yes, you do. An appointment like that is a day that will live in infamy, or that's how I see it."

"Don't jump to conclusions."

"No jumps. Just hopping mad. Or *will* be if you don't come clean."

"Is this supposed to be my second confession of the day?" She blinked.

"My God," I said, feeling an invisible stomach punch. "So that's it! You came plunging out of the confessional an hour ago and the first person you called with the lunatic news—"

"I didn't *plunge* out!"

"No, I suppose not. How long were you cooped up in there?"

"Not long."

"*How* long?"

"Half an hour. An hour."

"Is Reilly, Father Reilly taking a nap now? He *must*. How many dozen years of sin did you unload? Did he slip a word in edgewise? Was God mentioned?"

"Don't joke."

"Did that *sound* like a joke? So you trapped him for an hour, did you? I bet he's chugalugging the altar wine right now."

"Stop it!" she cried, and there were tears in her eyes. "I call you with good news and you spoil it."

"How long ago did you make this appointment with Reilly, *Father*, that is? Your first appointment, for instruction. It must take weeks or months. He does most of the talking, right, at the start?"

"Most."

"I'd just like to know the date is all. Is that asking too much?"

"January fifteenth, a Tuesday. Four o'clock."

I figured swiftly, sending my mind back. "Ah, yes," I said, and closed my eyes.

"Ah, yes, what?" She leaned forward.

"That was the last Tuesday, the final time you asked me to marry you."

"Was it?"

"Asked me to leave my wife and kids and marry you, yes."

"I don't recall."

"Yes, you do. And you recall my answer. No. Just

like the dozen other times. No. So you picked up the phone and called Reilly."

"It wasn't all that quick."

"No? Did you wait half an hour, forty-five minutes?"

She lowered her eyes. "An hour, maybe two."

"Let's say an hour and a half, split the difference, and he had the time and you went over. A glad hand for the Baptist. Jesus, Mary, and Moses. Give me that."

I grabbed the wine back and did away with my third glass.

"Shoot," I said, looking up at her.

"That's all," she said, simply.

"You mean you brought me all the way over here just to tell me you are a practicing Catholic and have unloaded fifteen years of accumulated guilt?"

"Well—"

"I'm waiting for the other shoe to drop."

"Shoe?"

"That glass slipper I slipped on your foot three years back, the one that fit so perfectly. When it drops it'll break. I'll be on my feet till midnight picking up the pieces."

"You're not going to cry, are you?" She leaned forward, peering into my face.

"Yes, no. I haven't decided. If I did, would you put me over your shoulder, like you always do, and burp me? You always did that and made me well. Now what?"

"You said it all."

"How come I thought I was waiting for you to say it? Say it."

"The priest said—"

"I don't want to hear what the priest said. Don't blame him. What do *you* say?"

"The priest said," she went on, as if not hearing me, "since I am now a member of his flock, that from now on I mustn't have anything to do with married men."

"What about *un*married men, what did he say about those?"

"We only talked 'married.' "

"Now we've almost got it. What you are saying is that . . ." I figured swiftly, counting back. "Is that the Tuesday before the Tuesday before last was our last tossing-the-blanket pillow fight?"

"I guess so," she said, miserably.

"You *guess* so?"

"Yes," she said.

"And I'm not to see you again?"

"We can have lunch—"

"Lunch, after all those midnight banquets and delicatessen-appetite-inducing brunches and made-in-heaven snacks?"

"Don't exaggerate."

"Exaggerate? Hell, I've lived inside a tornado for three incredible years and never touched ground. There wasn't a hair of my body that didn't throw sparks if you touched me. I no sooner got out your door with the sun going down every Tuesday than I wanted to charge back in and rip the paper off the walls, crying your name. Exaggerate? Exaggerate! Call the mad-house. Rent me a room!"

"You'll get over it," she said, lamely.

"Around about next July, maybe August. By Hal-loween I'll be a basket case . . . So from now on, Helen, you'll be seeing this Reilly, this father, this priest?"

"I don't like you putting it that way."

"He'll be instructing you every Tuesday afternoon, right as rain, on the nose? Well, will he or *won't* he?"

"Yes."

"My God!" I got up and walked around, talking to the walls. "What a plot for a book, a movie, a TV sit-com. Woman, lacking courage, no guts, figures amaz-ingly clever way to ditch her boyfriend. Can't just say, Out, go, be gone. No. Can't say, It's over, it was nice but it's over. No, sir. So she takes instruction and gets religion and uses the religion to call a halt and regain her virginity."

"That's not the way it was."

"You mean to say you just happened to get religion and once you were inoculated it suddenly struck you to call the Goodwill to come get me?"

"I never—"

"Yes, you did. And it's a perfect out. There's no way around it. I'm trapped. My hands are tied. If I forced you to love me now, you'd be sinning against Reilly's good advice. Lord, what a situation!"

I sat down again.

"Did you mention my name?"

"Not your *name*, no . . ."

"But you did talk about me, right? Hours and hours?"

"Ten minutes, maybe fifteen."

"How I was good at this and that and you couldn't bear to live without me?"

"I'm living without you now and free as a bird!"

"I can tell by that fake laugh."

"It's not fake. You just don't want to *hear* it."

"Continue."

"What?"

"Go on with your grocery list."

"That's all."

She laced and unlaced her fingers.

"Well, one other thing . . ."

"What?"

She took out a tissue and blew her nose.

"Every time we made love, it hurt."

"What?" I cried, stunned.

"It did," she said, not looking at me. "From the start. Always."

"You mean to say," I gasped, "that every time we took a trip to the moon on gossamer wings, it was *painful?*"

"Yes."

"And all those shouts and cries of joy were cover-ups for your discomfort?"

"Yes."

"All those *years*, all those *hours*, why didn't you *tell* me?"

"I didn't want to make you unhappy."

"Good God!" I cried.

And then, "I don't believe you."

"It's true."

"I don't believe you," I said, fighting to control my breath. "It was too wonderful, it was too great, it was— no, no, you couldn't have lied each time, every time." I stopped and stared at her. "You're making this up to tie it in with this Father Reilly thing. That's it, isn't it?"

"Honest to God—"

"Watch it. You're certified now! That's *blasphemy!*"

"Just *'honest'* then. No lie."

I lapsed back into hot confusion.

There was a long silence.

"We could still have lunch," she said. "Someday."

"No thanks. I couldn't stand it. To see you and have to sit across from you and not touch, oh, Lord! Where's my hat? Was I *wearing* one?"

I put my hand on the doorknob.

"Where are you going?" she cried.

I shook my head, eyes shut. "I don't know. Yes, I do. To join the Unitarian Church!"

"What?"

"Unitarians. *You* know."

"But you can't do *that!*"

"Why?"

"Because—"

"Because?"

"They never mention God or Jesus. They're embarrassed if you talk about them."

"Right."

"Which means, when I see you *I* wouldn't be able to mention God or Jesus."

"Right."

"You *wouldn't* join them!"

"No? You made the first move. Now it's mine. Checkmate."

I turned the doorknob and said:

"I'll call you next Tuesday, a last time. But if I do, don't ask me to marry you."

"Don't call," she said.

"Oh, love that I still dearly love," I said, "good-bye."

I went out and shut the door. Quietly.

Mr. Pale

"**H**e's a very sick man."

"Where is he?"

"Up above on Deck C. I got him to bed."

The doctor sighed. "I came on this trip for a vacation. All right, all right. Excuse me," he said to his wife. He followed the private up through the ramps of the spaceship and the ship, in the few minutes while he did this, pushed itself on in red and yellow fire across space, a thousand miles a second.

"Here we are," said the orderly.

The doctor turned in at the portway and saw the man lying on the bunk, and the man was tall and his flesh was sewed tight to his skull. The man was sick, and his lips fluted back in pain from his large, discolored teeth. His eyes were shadowed cups from which flickers of light peered, and his body was as thin as a skeleton. The color of his hands was that of snow. The doctor pulled up a magnetic chair and took the sick man's wrist.

"What seems to be the trouble?"

The sick man didn't speak for a moment, but only licked a colorless tongue over his sharp lips.

"I'm dying," he said, at last, and seemed to laugh.

"Nonsense, we'll fix you up, Mr. . . .?"

"Pale, to fit my complexion. Pale will do."

"Mr. Pale." This wrist was the coldest wrist he had ever touched in his life. It was like the hand of a body you pick up and tag in the hospital morgue. The pulse was gone from the cold wrist already. If it was there at all, it was so faint that the doctor's own fingertips, pulsing, covered it.

"It's bad, isn't it?" asked Mr. Pale.

The doctor said nothing but probed the bared chest of the dying man with his silver stethoscope.

There was a faint far clamor, a sigh, a musing upon distant things, heard in the stethoscope. It seemed almost to be a regretful wailing, a muted screaming of a million voices, instead of a heartbeat, a dark wind blowing in a dark space and the chest cold and the sound cold to the doctor's ears and to his own heart, which gave pause in hearing it.

"I was right, wasn't I?" said Mr. Pale.

The doctor nodded. "Perhaps you can tell me . . ."

"What caused it?" Mr. Pale closed his eyes smilingly over his colorlessness. "I haven't any food. I'm starving."

"We can fix that."

"No, no, you don't understand," whispered the man. "I barely made it to this rocket in time to get aboard. Oh, I was really healthy there for awhile, a few minutes ago.''

The doctor turned to the orderly. "Delirious.''

"No,'' said Mr. Pale, "no.''

"What's going on here?'' said a voice, and the captain stepped into the room. "Hello, who's this? I don't recall . . .''

"I'll save you the trouble,'' said Mr. Pale. "I'm not on the passenger list. I just came aboard.''

"You couldn't have. We're ten million miles away from Earth.''

Mr. Pale sighed. "I almost didn't make it. It took all my energy to catch you. If you'd been a little farther out . . .''

"A stowaway, pure and simple,'' said the captain. "And drunk, too, no doubt.''

"A very sick man,'' said the doctor. "He can't be moved. I'll make a thorough examination . . .''

"You'll find nothing,'' said Mr. Pale, faintly, lying white and long and alone in the cot, "except I'm in need of food.''

"We'll see about that,'' said the doctor, rolling up his sleeves.

An hour passed. The doctor sat back down on his magnetic chair. He was perspiring. "You're right. There's nothing wrong with you, except you're starved. How could you do this to yourself in a rich civilization like ours?''

"Oh, you'd be surprised,'' said the cold, thin, white man. His voice was a little breeze blowing ice through the room. "They took all my food away an hour or so ago. It was my own fault. You'll understand in a few minutes now. You see, I'm very very old. Some say a million years, some say a billion. I've lost count. I've been too busy to count."

Mad, thought the doctor, utterly mad.

Mr. Pale smiled weakly as if he had heard this thought. He shook his tired head and the dark pits of his eyes flickered. "No, no. No, no. Old, very old. And foolish. Earth was mine. I owned it. I kept it for myself. It nurtured me, even as I nurtured it. I lived well there, for a billion years, I lived high. And now here I am, in the name of all that's darkest, dying too. I never thought I could die. I never thought I could be killed, like everyone else. And now *I* know what the fear is, what it will be like to die. After a billion years I know, and it is frightening, for what will the universe be without me?"

"Just rest easily, now, we'll fix you up."

"No, no. No, no, there's nothing you can do. I overplayed my hand. I lived as I pleased. I started wars and stopped wars. But this time I went too far, and committed suicide, yes, I did. Go to the port there and look out." Mr. Pale was trembling, the trembling moved in his fingers and his lips. "Look out. Tell me what you see."

"Earth. The planet Earth, behind us."

"Wait just a moment, then," said Mr. Pale.

The doctor waited.

"Now," said Mr. Pale, softly. "It should happen about *now*."

A blind fire filled the sky.

The doctor cried out. "My God, my God, this is terrible!"

"What do you see?"

"Earth! It's caught fire. It's burning!"

"Yes," said Mr. Pale.

The fire crowded the universe with a dripping blue yellow flare. Earth blew itself into a thousand pieces and fell away into sparks and nothingness.

"Did you see?" said Mr. Pale.

"My God, my God." The doctor staggered and fell against the port, clawing at his heart and his face. He began to cry like a child.

"You see," said Mr. Pale, "what a fool I was. Too far. I went too far. I thought, What a feast. What a banquet. And now, and now, it's over."

The doctor slid down and sat on the floor, weeping. The ship moved in space. Down the corridors, faintly, you could hear running feet and stunned voices, and much weeping.

The sick man lay on his cot, saying nothing, shaking his head slowly back and forth, swallowing convulsively. After five minutes of trembling and weeping, the doctor gathered himself and crawled and then got to his feet and sat on the chair and looked at Mr. Pale who lay gaunt and long there, almost phosphorescent, and from the dying man came a thick smell of something very old and chilled and dead.

"Now do you see?" said Mr. Pale. "I didn't want it this way."

"Shut up."

"I wanted it to go on for another billion years, the high life, the picking and choosing. Oh, I was king."

"You're mad!"

"Everyone feared me. And now *I'm* afraid. For there's no one left to die. A handful on this ship. A few thousand left on Mars. That's why I'm trying to get there, to Mars, where I can live, if I make it. For in order for me to live, to be talked about, to have an existence, others must be alive to die, and when all the living ones are dead and no one is left to die, then Mr. Pale himself must die, and he most assuredly does not want that. For you see, life is a rare thing in the universe. Only Earth lived, and only I lived there because of the living men. But now I'm so weak, so weak. I can't move. You must help me."

"Mad, mad!"

"It's another two days to Mars," said Mr. Pale, thinking it through, his hands collapsed at his sides. "In that time you must feed me. I can't move or I would tend myself. Oh, an hour ago, I had great power, think of the power I took from so much and so many dying at once. But the effort of reaching this ship dispersed the power, and the power is self-limiting. For now I have no reason to live, except you, and your wife, and the twenty other passengers and crew, and those few on Mars. My incentive, you see, weakens, weakens . . ." His voice trailed off into a sigh. And then, after swallowing, he went on, "Have you wondered, Doctor, why the death rate on Mars in the six months since you established bases there has been nil? I can't be everywhere. I was born on Earth on the same day as life was born. And I've waited all these years to move on out into the star system. I should have gone months ago, but I put it off, and now, I'm sorry. What a fool, what a greedy fool."

The doctor stood up, stiffening and pulling back. He clawed at the wall. "You're out of your head."

"Am I? Look out the port again at what's left of Earth."

"I won't listen to you."

"You must help me. You must decide quickly. I want the captain. He must come to me first. A transfusion, you might call it. And then the various passengers, one by one, just to keep me on the edge, to keep me alive. And then, of course, perhaps even you, or your wife. You don't want to live forever, do you? That's what would happen if you let me die."

"You're raving."

"Do you dare believe I am raving? Can you take that chance? If I die, all of you would be immortal. That's what man's always wanted, isn't it? To live forever. But I tell you, it would be insanity, one day like another, and think of the immense burden of memory! Think! Consider."

The doctor stood across the room with his back to the wall, in shadow.

Mr. Pale whispered, "Better take me up on this. Better die when you have the chance than live on for a million billion years. Believe me. I *know*. I'm almost glad to die. Almost, but not quite. Self-preservation. Well?"

The doctor was at the door. "I don't believe you."

"Don't go," murmured Mr. Pale. "You'll regret it."

"You're lying."

"Don't let me die . . ." The voice was so far away now, the lips barely moved. "Please don't let me die. You need me. All life needs me to make life worthwhile, to give it value, to give it contrast. Don't . . ."

Mr. Pale was thinner and smaller and now the flesh seemed to melt faster. "No," he sighed. "No . . ." said the wind behind the hard yellowed teeth. "Please . . ." The deep-socketed eyes fixed themselves in a stare at the ceiling.

The doctor crashed out the door and slammed it and bolted it tight. He lay against it, weeping again, and through the ship he could see the people standing in groups staring back at the empty space where Earth had been. He heard cursing and wailing. He walked unsteadily and in great unreality for an hour through the ship's corridors until he reached the captain.

"Captain, no one is to enter that room where the dying man is. He has a plague. Incurable. Quite insane. He'll be dead within the hour. Have the room welded shut."

"What?" said the captain. "Oh, yes, yes. I'll attend to it. I will. Did you see? See Earth go?"

"I saw it."

They walked numbly away from each other. The doctor sat down beside his wife who did not recognize him for a moment until he put his arm around her.

"Don't cry," he said. "Don't cry. Please don't cry."

Her shoulders shook. He held her very tightly, his eyes clenched in on the trembling in his own body. They sat this way for several hours.

"Don't cry," he said. "Think of something else. Forget Earth. Think about Mars, think about the future."

They sat back in their seats with vacant faces. He lit a cigarette and could not taste it, and passed it to her and lit another for himself. "How would you like to be married to me for another ten million years?" he asked.

"Oh, I'd like that," she cried out, turning to him and seizing his arm in her own, fiercely wrapping it to her. "I'd like that very much!"

"*Would* you?" he said.

That Bird That Comes
Out of the Clock

"**Y**ou remember people by the things they do," said Mrs. Coles, "rather than by how their face looks or what their tongues say, while they're doing what they do. Now, if you ask me, this new woman across the street and down two houses, Kit Random, that her name? She is, to put it mildly, a woman of action."

Everybody on the porch looked.

There was Kit Random with a flower in her hand, in the garden. There she was drawing the shade in the upstairs window. There fanning herself in the cool dark doorway of her front porch. There making mosquito-delicate etchings under a lemon-colored hurricane lamp at night. There throwing clay on a potter's wheel early mornings, singing in a loud clear-water voice. There shoving dozens of ashtrays into a kiln she had built of bricks. And again you saw her baking pies for God knows who in her empty house and setting them to cool in windowsills so men on the far side of the street crossed over, noses lifted, passing. Then, when the sun set, she swung in a great hairy hemp swing she had tied to the vast oak in her backyard. About nine at night, carrying a crank phonograph like the white Victrola dog in her hands, she'd come out, crank up the machine, put on a record, and swing in the giant child's swing, being a poor butterfly or a red red robin hop hop hopping along.

"Yes," said Mrs. Tiece. "She's either a very shrewd woman up to her feminine tricks or—" And here she debated a moment. "She's that little bird that comes out of the clock . . . that little bird that comes out of the clock . . ."

All along the street, women tapped their heads with knowing forefingers and looked over her fence, like women peering over a cliff, ready to scream at how high up they were, but all they saw was the nine o'clock backyard, as dim as a cavern full of sprouting leaves, starred with flowers, the phonograph hissing and clearing its throat before launching itself down the grooves of "June Night" or "Poor Butterfly." And there, with the regularity of an unseen, but nevertheless ticking pendulum, back and forth, one arm up to cushion her pink little pillow of cheek, sighing quietly to herself, was Kit Random, swinging in her swing, in rhythm to the things the phonograph said were poor about the butterfly or nice about the June night.

"Where's she from?"

"No one knows."

"What's she doing here?"

"No one knows."

"How long's she going to stay?"

"Go ask *her!*"

The facts were simple enough. The house had been unrented for a year, and then it was rented. One April afternoon a large moving van drove up and two men ran in and out, like Keystone Cops, the nearest thing to collision, but always skidding around each other with a fast-action routine of clocks, lamps, chairs, tables, and urns. In what seemed a minute they had driven away. The house was left alone, unoccupied. Mrs. Coles had walked by it four times and peered in, and only seen that the moving men had hung the pictures, spread the rugs, adjusted the furniture, and made everything womanly and neat before they had come running out to go away. There was the nest, waiting for the bird.

And promptly at seven o'clock, just after supper, when everyone could see her, up drove Kit Random in a yellow taxicab, and moved into the waiting house, alone.

"Where's Mr. Random?" asked everyone.

"There isn't any."

"Divorced, that's what she is, divorced. Or maybe her husband dead. A widow, that's better. Poor thing."

But there was Kit Random smiling at every window and every porch, on her way to buy T-bone steaks, tomato soup, and dishwater soap, not looking tired, not looking sad, not looking alone, but looking as if a company of clowns lived with her by day, and a handsome film gentleman with a waxed mustache by night.

"But no one ever comes *near* her place. At first I thought, well . . ." Mrs. Coles hesitated. "A woman living alone. Oh, *you* know. But there hasn't even been an iceman close. So there's only one thing to figure: as someone said, she's that bird that comes out of the clock. Four times an hour," she added.

At that very moment, Miss Kit Random called to the ladies, now her voice up in the soft green trees, now up in the blue sky on the opposite side of the yard. "Ladies?"

Their heads twisted. Their ears prickled.

"Ladies," called Miss Kit Random, in flight. "I've come to get me a man. That's *it*, ladies!"

All the ladies backed off to their houses.

It was the next afternoon that they found Mr. Tiece over in Miss Kit Random's front yard playing marbles. Mrs. Tiece put up with it for about two minutes and thirty-five seconds and then came across the street, almost on roller skates.

"Well, what're we *doing*?" she demanded of the two hunched-down figures.

"Just a moment." A marble spun bright under Henry Tiece's thumb. Other marbles spat against each other and clacked away.

"Looks like you won," said Kit Random. "You're darned good at mibs, Hank."

"It's been years." Mr. Tiece glanced uneasily at his

wife's ankle. She had veins like runners of light blue ink on her legs. It looked like the map of Illinois. Desplaines River here, Mississippi there. He scanned up as far as Rock Island when his wife said:

"Isn't it a little strange playing marbles?"

"Strange *thing?*" Mr. Tiece dusted himself off. "I *won!*"

"What you going to do with them marbles?"

"It's not what I *do* with them, it's victory that *counts.*"

Mrs. Tiece glared at them as if they were toadstools. "Thanks for giving Henry a game."

"Anytime, Clara, anytime," said Kit Random.

"I'll just leave these with you." Henry handed over the marbles hastily. "No room at my place."

"I want you to cut the grass," said Mrs. Tiece.

He and Mrs. Tiece sort of walked across the street, he not looking at her, she keeping up so he walked faster, she increasing her pace, he increasing his until they almost leaped up the porch steps. He ran to the door first, she tailed after. The door-slam was such that birds abandoned their nests three houses down.

The next incident occurred exactly an hour later. Mr. Tiece was out mowing the lawn, his eyes fixed to the rotating machine and each of one hundred clover blossoms, all with tiny heads like Mrs. Tiece. He cut furiously east, west, north, south, perspiring and wiping his brow as Mrs. Tiece shouted, "Don't miss the outer drive! And down the middle, you missed a ridge. Watch that stone, you'll ruin the cutter!"

Exactly at two o'clock two trucks drove up in front of Miss Kit Random's house and a couple of laborers began tossing dirt out of Miss Random's lawn. By four o'clock they poured a solid sheet of cement all over Miss Random's yard.

At five o'clock, the truck drove off, taking Miss Kit Random's lawn with it, at which point Miss Kit Random waved over to Mr. Tiece. "Won't have to mow this lawn again for a couple years I guess!" She laughed.

Mr. Tiece started to laugh back when he sensed someone hidden inside the dark screen door. Mr. Tiece ducked inside. This time, with the door-slam, two potted geraniums fell off the porch rail.

"The nerve of that woman."

"Did it on purpose."

"Trying to make us look like slave drivers. Putting cement over her lawn. Giving Mr. Tiece ideas. Well, we're not cementing *our* lawn, he'll cut it every week, or my name isn't Clara Moon Tiece!"

The three ladies snorted over their knitting.

"Seems like some sort of plot to me," said Mrs. Coles. "Look at her backyard, a jungle, nothing in its right place."

"Tell us about the marble game again, Clara."

"Good grief. There he was down on his knees, both laughing. I—wait a minute. You *hear* something?"

It was twilight, just after supper, and the three

women on Mrs. Coles' porch right next door. "That Clock Woman's out in her backyard again, laughing."

"Swinging in her swing?"

"Listen. Shh!"

"I haven't done this in *years!*" a man's voice laughed. "Always wanted to, but folks think you're crazy! Hey!"

"Who's that?" cried Mrs. Coles.

The three women clapped their hands to their thumping chests and lurched to the far end of the porch, panicked excursioners on a sinking ship.

"Here you go!" cried Kit Random, giving a push.

And there in her backyard going up in the green leaves one way, then down and swooping up on the other, in the twilight air was a laughing man.

"Don't that sound a bit like your Mr. Coles?" one of the ladies wondered.

"The idea!"

"Oh, Fanny."

"The *idea!*"

"Oh, Fanny, go to sleep," said Mr. Coles in bed. The room was warm and dark. She sat like a great lump of ice cream glowing in the dim room at eleven o'clock.

"Ought to be run out of town."

"Oh, for God's sake." He punched his pillow. "It was just a backyard swing, haven't swung in years. Big damn swing, plenty hefty to ride a man. You left me to finish the dishes so you could go out and blather with those hens, I went to toss out the garbage and there she was swinging in the swing and I said how nice it looked and she said did I want to try? So, by God, I just climbed over to pump myself up for a ride."

"And cackling like an idiot rooster."

"Not cackling, damn it, but laughing. I wasn't pinching her behind, was I?" He punched his pillow twice more and rolled over.

In his sleep she heard him mumble, "Best damn swing I ever swung," which set her off into a new fit of weeping.

It remained only for Mr. Clements to jump off the cliff the next afternoon. Mrs. Clements found him blowing bubbles on Miss Kit Random's back garden wall, discussing the formation, clarity, and coloration of same with her. Her phonograph was warbling an old tune from World War I sung by the Knickerbocker Quartet titled "The Worst Is Yet to Come." Mrs. Clements acted out the song's words by grabbing Mr. Clements by the ear and lugging him off.

"That woman's yard," said Mrs. Coles, Mrs. Clements, and Mrs. Tiece, "is, as of this hour, day, and minute, forbidden territory."

"Yes, dear," said Mr. Coles, Mr. Clements, and Mr. Tiece.

"You are not to say good morning or good night, Nurse, to her," said Mrs. Coles, Mrs. Clements, and Mrs. Tiece.

"Of course not, dear," said the husbands behind their newspapers.

"You *hear* me?"

"Yes, sweetheart," came the chorus.

From then on Mr. Coles, Mr. Clements, and Mr. Tiece could be seen mowing lawns, fixing lights, trimming hedges, painting doors, cleaning windows, washing dishes, digging bulbs, watering trees, fertilizing flowers, rushing to work, rushing back, bending, flexing, running, pausing, reaching, busy at a thousand and one tasks with a thousand and one perspirations.

Whereas in Kit Random's clocks had stopped, flowers died or went insane with abundance. Doorknobs fell off if you tapped them, trees shed their leaves in mid-summer for lack of water; paint flaked from doors, and the electric light-system, burnt out, was replaced with candles rammed in wine jugs: a paradise of neglect, a beautiful chaos.

Somewhere along the line Mrs. Coles, Mrs. Clements and Mrs. Tiece were stunned at the pure unadulterated nerve of Kit Random shoving notes in their mailboxes during the night, inviting them to come by at four next day for poisoned tea.

They absolutely refused.

And *went.*

Kit Random poured them all the orange pekoe which was her favorite and then sat back, smiling.

"It was nice of you ladies to come," she said.

The ladies nodded grimly.

"There's a lot for us to talk about," she added.

The ladies waited stone-cold, leaning toward the door.

"I feel you don't understand me at all," said Kit Random. "I feel I must explain everything."

They waited.

"I'm a maiden lady with a private income."

"Looks *suspiciously* private to me," observed Mrs. Tiece.

"Suspiciously," echoed Mrs. Cole.

Mrs. Clements was about to toss her teabag in the cup when Kit Random uncorked a laugh.

"I can see no matter what I say you'll add sugar lumps and stir your spoons so loud I can't be heard."

"Try us," said Mrs. Tiece.

Kit Random reached over to pick up a shiny brass tube and twist it.

"What's *that?*" asked all three at once and then covered their mouths as if embarrassed not one of them had said anything original.

"One of them toy kaleidoscopes." Kit Random shut one eye to squint through the odd-colored shards. "Right now I'm examining your gizzards. Know what I *find?*"

"How could we possibly care?" cried Mrs. Clements. The others nodded at her snappy retort.

"I see a solid potato." Kit Random fixed the device to X-ray Mrs. Tiece, then moved to the others. "A rutabaga and a nice round turnip. No innards, stomach, spleen, or heart. I've listened. No pulse, just solid flesh, fit to burst your corsets. And your tongues? Not connected to your cerebral cortex . . ."

"Our cerebral *what?*" cried Mrs. Tiece, offended.

"*Cortex*. Not as off-color as it sounds. And I've made a brave decision. Don't get up."

The three women squirmed in their chairs and Kit Random said:

"I'm going to take your husbands, one by one. I'm going to, in the words of the old song, steal their hearts away. Or what's there if you left any on the plate. I've decided that flimsy-whimsy as I am, I'll be a darn sight better midnight or high-noon companion than all of you in a bunch. Don't speak, don't leave. I'm almost done. There's nothing you can do to stop me. Oh, yes, one thing. Love these fine men. But I don't think it crossed your minds, it's so long ago. Look at their faces. See how they crush their straw hats down hard over their ears and grind their teeth in their sleep. Heck, I can hear it way over *here!* And make fists when they walk, with no one to hit. So stand back, don't even try to interfere. And how will I do it? With cribbage and dead man's poker, and miniature golf in my garden, I'll pull flowers to sink par-three holes. Then there's blackjack, dominoes, checkers, chess, beer and ice cream, hot dogs noons, hamburgers midnights, phonograph moonlight dancing, fresh beds, clean linens, singing in the shower allowed, litter all week, clean up on Sundays, grow a mustache or beard, go barefoot at croquet. When the beer stops, gin stays. Hold on! Sit!"

Kit Random lectured on:

"I can see what you think, you got faces like sieves. No, I'm not the Hoor of Babylon, nor the Tart from Le Petit Trianon, which, incidentally, is *not* a movie-house.

I am a traveling Jungle Gym, first cousin to a sideshow, never a beauty, almost a freak. But one day years back, I decided not to make *one* man sad but a *handful* happy! I found I was trying to win all the time, which is an error beyond most women's imagination. If you make a man lose all the time, hell, he'll go play golf or hand-ball and lose *right.* At least he can add it *up!* So I started out, two years in Placerville, three in Tallahassee and Kankakee until I ran out of steam or my rolling stock rusted. What was my great secret? Not playing Par-cheesi, or Uncle Wiggily says jump back three hops to the henhouse, no. It was *losing.* Don't you *see?* I learned how to cheat and lose. Men *like* that. They know what you're up to, sure, but pretend not to notice and the more you lose the more they love. Next thing you know you got 'em bound head and foot with just plain old self-destruction pinochle or I'm-dead-send-flowers hop-scotch. You can get a man to jump rope if you convince him he's the greatest jumper since the Indian rope trick. So you go on losing and find you've won all along as the men tip their hat to you at breakfast, put down the stock-market quotes and *talk!*

"Stop fidgeting! I'm almost out of gas. Will you get your halfway loved ones back? Mebbe. Mebbe not. A year from now I'll check to see if you've watched and learned from my show-and-tell. I'll give you the loan of those lost but now found souls and once a year after that bus back through to see if you're losing proper in order to learn to laugh. Meanwhile, there's nothing you can do, starting this very second. Now, consider I've just fired off a gun. Go home. Bake pies. Make meat-balls. But it won't work. The pies will fall flat and the meatballs? Dead on arrival. Because you arm-wrestle them to the table and spoil men's appetites. And don't lock your doors. Let the poor beasts run. Like you've excused."

"We've just begun to fight!" cried all three and then, confused at their echoes, almost fell down the porch stairs.

Well, that was the true end. There was no war, not even a battle or half a skirmish. Every time the ladies glanced around they found empty rooms and quietly shut on tiptoes front doors.

But what really scalded the cat and killed the dog was when three strange men showed up half-seen in the twilight one late afternoon and caused the wives to pull back, double-lock their doors, and peer through their lace curtains.

"Okay, open up!" the three men cried.

And hearing voices from today's breakfast, the wives unlocked the doors to squint out.

"Henry Tiece?"

"Robert Joe Clements, what—?"

"William Ralph Cole, is that *you?*"

"Who the hell do you *think* it is!"

Their wives stood back to watch the almost hairless wonders pass.

"My God," said Mrs. Tiece.

"What?" said Mrs. Clements.

"What have you done to your hair?"

"Nothing," said all three husbands. "*She* did."

The wives circled their relatives by marriage.

"I didn't recognize you," gasped Mrs. Tiece.

"You weren't *supposed* to!"

And so said all the rest.

Adding, "How you *like* it?"

"It's not the man I married," they said.

"Damn tootin'!"

And at last, almost in chorus, though in separate houses:

"You going to change your *name* to fit the *haircut?*"

The last night of the month, Mr. Tiece was found in his upper-stairs bedroom packing a grip. Mrs. Tiece clutched a doorknob and held on. "Where you going?"

"Business."

"Where?"

"A ways."

"Going to be gone long?"

"Hard to say," he said, packing a shirt.

"Two days?" she asked.

"Maybe."

"Three days?"

"Where's my blue necktie? The one with the white mice on it."

"I never did like that necktie."

"Would you mind finding the blue necktie with the white mice on it for me?"

She found it.

"Thank you." He knotted it, watching himself in the

252

mirror. He brushed his hair and grimaced to see if he had brushed his teeth.

"*Four* days?" she asked.

"In all probability," he said.

"A *week* then?" She smiled wildly.

"You can almost bet on it," he said, examining his fingernails.

"Eat good meals now, not just quick sandwiches."

"I promise."

"Get plenty of sleep!"

"I'll get plenty of sleep."

"And be sure to phone every night. Have you got your stomach pills with you?"

"Won't need the stomach pills."

"You've *always* needed the stomach pills." She ran to fetch them. "Now, you just take these stomach pills."

He took and put them in his pocket. He picked up his two suitcases.

"And be sure and call me every night," she said.

He went downstairs with her after.

"And don't sit in any draughts."

He kissed her on the brow, opened the front door, went out, shut the door.

At almost the same instant, so it couldn't have been coincidence, Mr. Cole and Mr. Clements plunged, blind with life, off their front porches, risking broken legs or ankles to be free, and raced out to mid-street where they all but collided with Mr. Tiece.

They glanced at each other's faces and luggage and in reverberative echoes cried:

"Where're you going?"

"What's *that?*"

"My suitcase."

"My valise."

"My overnight case!"

"Do you realize this is the first time we've met in the middle of the street since Halloween twenty years ago?"

"Hell, this *is* Halloween!"

"Yeah! For what? Trick or treat?"

"Let's go see!"

And unerringly, with no chart, map, or menu, they turned with military abruptness and headlong sparked Kit Random's yardwide cement with their heels.

In the next week the sounds that abounded in Kit Random's abode might as well have been a saloon bowling alley. In just a handful of days, three various husbands visited at nine, ten, then ten after midnight, all with smiles like fake celluloid teeth hammered in place. The various wives checked their breaths for liquid sustenance but inhaled only tart doses of medicinal mint; the men wisely gargled mid-street before charging up to confront their fortress Europas.

As for the disdained and affronted wives, what culinary battlements did they rear up? What counterattacks ensued? And if small battles, or skirmishes, were fought, did victories follow?

The problem was that the husbands backing off and then headlong racing off let all of the hot air out of their houses. Only cold air remained, with three ladies delivered out of ice floes, refrigerated in their corsets, stony of glance and smile that in delivering victuals to the table caused frost to gather on the silverware. Hot roast beef became tough icebox leftovers two minutes from the oven. As the husbands glanced sheepishly up from their now more infrequent meals, they were greeted with displays of glass eyes like those in the optician's downtown window at midnight, and smiles that echoed fine porcelain when they opened and shut to let out what should have been laughter but was pure death rattle.

And then at last a night came when three dinners were laid on three tables by candlelight and no one came home and the candles snuffed out all by themselves, while across the way the sound of horseshoes clanking the stake or, if you really listened close, taffy being pulled, or Al Jolson singing, "Hard-hearted Hannah, the vamp of Savannah, I don't mean New Orleans," made the three wives count the cutlery, sharpen the knives, and drink Lydia Pinkham's Female Remedy long before the sun was over the yardarm.

But the last straw that broke the camel herd was the men ducking through a whirlaround garden sprinkler one untimely hot autumn night and, seeing their wives in a nearby window, they yelled, "Come on *in*, the water's *fine!*"

All three ladies gave the window a grand slam.

Which knocked *five* flowerpots off rails, skedaddled six cats, and had ten dogs howling at no-moon-in-the-sky halfway to dawn.

A Brief Afterword

In a long life I have never had a driver's license nor have I learned to drive. But some while back one night I dreamed that I was motoring along a country road with my inspirational Greek muse. She occupied the driver's seat while I occupied the passenger's place with a second, student's, wheel.

I could not help but notice that she was driving, serenely, with a clean white blindfold over her eyes, while her hands barely touched the steering wheel.

And as she drove she whispered notions, concepts, ideas, immense truths, fabulous lies, which I hastened to jot down.

A time finally came, however, when, curious, I reached over and nabbed the edge of her blindfold to peer beneath.

Her eyes, like the eyes of an ancient statue, were rounded pure white marble. Sightless, they stared at the road ahead, which caused me, in panic, to seize *my* wheel and almost run us off the road.

"No, no," she whispered. "Trust me. I know the way."

"But I don't," I cried.

"It's all right," she whispered. "You don't need to know. If you must touch the wheel, remember Hamlet's advice, 'Use all gently.' Close your eyes. Now, quietly, reach out."

I did. *She* did. "There, *see?*" she whispered. "We're almost there."

We arrived. And all of the tales in this new book were finished and done.

"Night Train to Babylon" is an almost true story; I was nearly tossed off a train some years ago for interfering with a three-card monte scam. After that, I shut my mouth.

"That Old Dog Lying in the Dust" is an absolutely accurate detailing of an encounter I had with a Mexican border-town one-ring circus when I was twenty-four years old. A dear-sad evening I will remember to the end of my life.

"Nothing Changes" was triggered when one afternoon in the twilight stacks of Acres of Books in Long Beach I came upon a series of 1905 high school annuals in which (impossible) the faces of my own 1938 school chums seemed to appear again and again. Rushing from the stacks, I wrote the story.

"If MGM Is Killed, Who Gets the Lion?" is another variation on an amusing reality. During World War II MGM was camouflaged as the Hughes Aircraft Company, while the Hughes Aircraft Company was disguised as MGM. How could I *not* describe the comedy?

Finally, "Driving Blind" is a remembrance of my acquaintance with a Human Fly who climbed building facades when I was twelve. You don't find heroes like that by the dozen.

As you can see, when the Muse speaks, I shut my eyes and listen. In Paris once, I touch-typed in a dark room, no lights, and wrote 150 pages of a novel in seventeen nights without seeing what I put down. If that isn't Driving Blind, what is?

Ray Bradbury
Los Angeles
April 8, 1997

Copyright Notices